AMALFITANO'S
BOLD ABDUCTION

(AN ITALIAN BILLIONAIRES NOVEL)

Jennifer

Blake

STEEL MAGNOLIA PRESS

THE AMALFITANO'S BOLD ABDUCTION

ISBN: 9781519085122

ONE

*I*t just had to happen.

Dana Marsden had been expecting to come upon an accident or traffic jam for the past dozen white-knuckle miles. Italy's Amalfi Coast was breathtaking with its mountain and sea vistas and villages clinging to rocky ledges, but rain and early morning fog turned its winding road into a potential disaster zone.

Seeing a problem ahead as her small rental car topped a rise and started down gave her no satisfaction. She always hoped people would surprise her.

She hit the brake, easing the light-weight mini onto the shoulder as much as possible while showing a healthy respect for the rocky cliff that fell away behind the low cream-colored stone guard wall. She didn't like the steep incline she was on, but what could she do? With the mountain's solid rock face on one side and a sheer drop to the richly blue Mediterranean on the other, there was literally nowhere else to go.

Through clapping wipers and the raindrops that spattered her windshield, she assessed the situation ahead. The road narrowed as it rounded a curve. A big Mercedes tourist bus traveling in the same direction she was headed had stopped just inside this curve as it met a white delivery van coming from the opposite direction. There wasn't enough room for the two vehicles to pass each other in the sharp bend.

The bus driver would normally have seen the van coming in the traffic mirror on its post and pulled over in the lay-by for it to pass. The rain and drifting fog must have decreased visibility so he was in the curve before he spotted the van. Both drivers had come to a halt.

The standoff could have been easily remedied except an impatient driver in a Citroen had tried to pass the delivery van on the inside of the curve. He failed to make it, and was now stuck between the van and the stone wall. Another car had piled in behind him, preventing either the Citroen or the van from reversing.

Meanwhile, two other cars were lined up behind the tourist bus, as well as the silver and black Lamborghini Aventador which idled just ahead of her vehicle. This string of traffic, though not that long, made it impossible for the tourist bus to back up.

It was an impasse, and several of the drivers were using their horns in a noisy show of their displeasure.

What was required, Dana saw at once, was a traffic cop, or at least one of the *carabinieri* in their natty blue uniforms that she'd seen this morning in Naples. No such officials were anywhere in sight.

She sighed and rested her head on the steering wheel of her rental for an instant. She didn't need this, not in a foreign country where she spoke not a word of the language. She was on vacation, for Pete's sake; she'd left duty and too-dumb-to-live drivers behind. She was supposed to be enjoying herself, not clearing her thousandth traffic jam.

Moaning wasn't going to get her anywhere, and certainly not on her way to Positano. Dana straightened, set the emergency flashers and hand brake then turned off the engine. She got out and slammed the door, grimacing a little at the tinny sound of the bug of a car. She missed her half-ton truck already, and she'd only picked up the rental a short while ago.

She stood for an instant with the rain peppering down on her head. It was just what she needed, to get wet. Not that it would be the first time in the line of duty, of course, but it irked her anyway. She liked to be prepared, had almost thrown a slicker and umbrella into her suitcase. But who brought things like that to sunny Italy in August? Suzanne and Caryn had thought the idea was hysterical.

Her friends left the States three days ago so were probably blissfully relaxed at the house the three of them were renting for the next two weeks. Suzanne called the place a romantic villa, and had been in ecstasy over its grand view of the Mediterranean. Dana figured it would turn out to be just a house, with the only way they'd glimpse the sea being to hang out an upstairs window and squint. As for lying around the community pool catching rays, that wasn't happening any time soon. The rain was light but steady, and the fog that shifted in cloud-like banks, creeping up from the dark blue surface of the Mediterranean, touched her face with chill fingers.

It was also getting thicker by the minute, bringing with it a briny smell to go with the surrounding odors of exhaust and wet tarmac. She could barely see the bus up ahead now, and the Lamborghini was an indefinite gray shape in the drifting pall. Her footsteps slowed as she noticed movement, a dark shadow rising within the bank of white.

A car door slammed with the solid thud that signaled quality construction backed by mega-bucks. The figure of a man appeared, materializing out of the mist. A good five inches taller than her stately five-nine, he was broad shouldered, slim-hipped and carried himself with easy athletic grace. The cream cotton sweater he wore with the sleeves pushed to the elbows, the well-worn jeans and soft leather driving loafers, made him look as if he'd stepped from the pages of a European male fashion magazine. Chiseled, aristocratic features like those seen on antique coins topped off the impression. Fog and rain spangled the dark waves of his hair, and began to appear as damp splotches on the shoulders of his sweater.

Dana came to a halt while her heartbeat kicked it up a notch. The man faced her, perhaps alerted to her presence by her last grating footstep. The fog-dulled blare of car horns and hum of engines seemed to die away, leaving the quiet whisper of the sea far below where they stood.

For an endless moment, they watched each other there in the world of swirling white. She studied his straight nose, wide-spaced eyes with a hint of green, sensually molded mouth and square jaw as if she might need to pick him out of a future lineup. She might have stood there for ages if he hadn't drawn a swift breath, murmuring something that had the soft sibilance of an oath.

"Well, hi there."

It wasn't the most scintillating greeting she'd ever managed, but was better than staring as if she'd never seen a man before.

"*Buon giorno.* Your pardon, but you are English?" His voice was as entrancing as the rest of him, deep and vibrant with a fascinating accent that made her long to hear him say something else.

"American, born and bred." Her answer came out with precision as she shook off her unusual bemusement.

"But *naturalmente.* Naturally. It will be best if you |remain in your car. Who can say when someone may speed over the hill and not see you here on the roadway until it is too late."

Dana grinned, she couldn't help it. This good-looking Italian sounded so serious, so concerned and full of superior masculine knowledge. It was endearing in an annoying sort of way.

"You are out of your car," she pointed out.

"*Certo.* True. But I will hear them coming and step aside." His frown was a masterpiece of concern mixed with impatience.

"So will I, I promise."

He moved a step closer. "Perhaps. But there is nothing to be seen anyway. It is not a spectacle, but merely a great stupidity. I will settle the matter in a moment, and then we may be on our way."

He had a point, of course, one Dana had impressed on gawking drivers a bazillion times. Still, he was so earnest, so completely unconscious of the condescension in his voice, that she couldn't help playing along. "Will you now? And how is that?"

"The white van must be persuaded to reverse. The *idiota* who blocks progress in the curve should then drive forward and away. And the tourist bus must then advance, leaving the way clear for our progress."

Dana gave a decided shake of her head. "That won't work."

"Pardon?"

"Well, not without the delivery van crushing the car." It was amazing, the heat in his sage green eyes at the idea she might disagree with him. She loved it. If she had to see it every day, it would probably get old, but the sight jump-started an odd feeling inside her just now that was like euphoria.

"You are mistaken, I think."

She didn't bother to answer that. "Both the delivery van and the bus need to back up. Well, and the others in front of us here, of course. The man in the Citroen can then remove his vehicle without damage, after which the driver of the van can roll forward into the lay-by there against the rock.

When the way is clear, the bus and the rest of us here behind it can get back on the road."

He muttered something in his native tongue. She didn't know what he'd said and didn't much care, but enjoyed the sound of it anyway.

"You don't agree?" she asked with an air of innocence.

He folded his arms across his chest, a movement that flexed the muscles in his arms beneath the fine knit of his sweater with dramatic, almost breathtaking results. "In the first place, you will have to convince five drivers to reverse instead of two."

"You don't think I can?"

"You appear to have no Italian."

She gave him a crooked smile. "But I'm good at hand signals and some things are universal."

"They will pay no attention to you. They are not at fault and they know it."

"Are you counting yourself among those reluctant to back up when directed?"

"It makes no sense."

"It makes excellent sense. It's just that you don't want to admit it. Would that be because the suggestion comes from a mere female?"

His gaze drifted from her eyes to her mouth and down to her breasts under a T-shirt that said *Police Do It Politely* in navy blue lettering on white, then to her pressed jeans and brand new white sneakers. Something hot and more than a little disturbing spread over her from the places where his gaze had lingered.

"There is nothing "mere" about you."

She'd thought for a second he meant to say there was nothing female about her. It snapped her out of the odd trance that held her rooted on the roadside, talking to a strange man in the fog.

"Fine," she said, setting her hands on her hips. "And while we're standing arguing, traffic is piling up behind the van and we're both getting wet. I should tell you that I work as a traffic cop back in the States. Unsnarling jams like this is how I make my living. Now if you'll just get back in your fancy car and reverse the thing so the rest of the poor suckers can do the same, we can all get on our way."

"You are a policeman," he said, his voice flat.

"Policewoman, not that it matters. What counts here is—"

A yowl, ear-splitting and edged with desperation, came from out of the fog. As Dana swung toward the sound, something incredibly swift and furry hurtled toward her. It sank claws into the heavy denim of her jeans and then swarmed upward. It didn't stop until it was wrapped around her neck like a cowl.

The Italian exclaimed and reached for the creature. It hissed and swiped at his hand. He jerked it back, though barely in time to keep from being clawed. He knotted the hand into a fist as he scowled at the cat.

It was indeed a cat, Dana realized, though that was a little like saying a racing thoroughbred worth millions was a horse. This was an aristocrat among cats, a fluffy, meticulously brushed long-haired Siamese with the brown feet, face, ears and tail tip that marked it as a Seal Point. Tilting her chin to see better, she realized it was wearing a jeweled collar set with what appeared to be topaz stones the pure blue color of its eyes. It also had a smug, extremely self-satisfied expression.

"Well, aren't you a beauty," she crooned in soothing tones, mainly because the seal point was gripping the top of her shoulder in its distress. "And what's your name?"

"*HIS NAME IS Guaio*. You would say Trouble or, perhaps, Nuisance." The Italian raised his hands, reaching for the cat. "Here, let me have him."

The big feline sank his claws in, refusing to budge. Dana winced and hunched her shoulder, a decent cover for the shiver that ran over her at the electrifying brush of warm, masculine knuckles against her neck.

"Hold on a second," she said on a quick intake of breath. "Give him time to settle."

"You will be sorry. He could be there until noon."

"He's scared, I think, maybe because he's outside in a strange place."

"He is overjoyed to have escaped my car," the handsome Italian corrected. "He must have slipped out just now when I left the door open for a moment—I should have known better than to let him ride outside his carrier. Beyond this, he prefers women."

Dana gave him a quick glance. "You're joking."

"I wish I were."

"He'll be okay in a minute, and will probably go to you then. Meanwhile I have a job to do, so I'll just take him along with—"

"Wait," he said as she started to walk away. He raked his hand through his curling, rain-wet hair. "Very well. If you will look after Guaio for only a moment, I will instruct the drivers in the maneuver you suggested."

"Really?" It was ridiculous to be so gratified that he saw the advantage of her plan, or at least enough that he would carry through with it. She was usually more inclined to crow when a male colleague was forced to admit she was right.

She'd never been particularly susceptible to a handsome face. To discover she could be now was disturbing.

"*Certo*," he answered, his features grim as he sent a narrow glance up the road behind them and then back toward the stalled traffic. "The sooner we are away from here, the better."

~ ~ ~

The American woman was correct in her assessment of the situation; Andrea Tonello saw that clearly when he moved close enough for a better view through the fog. No doubt her assessment of the positions of both bus and van had been better from further uphill. He still doubted her ability to have carried out her plan, however. Not, *per Dio*, because she could not make herself understood but because the drivers of the stalled cars, being male and Italian, would have been too busy looking her over to pay attention to what she was saying.

He'd had much the same problem at first, this he had to admit. Her hair was so bright and silky-looking on this gray morning that she had to be a natural redhead, and he could hardly look away from her eyes that met his with such frank, shining humor. They were richly brown, yes, but had a gray outer ring that made them seem dark and deep enough that a man could become lost in them. Her features were alluring, her skin amazingly clear and her smile like sunshine on this gray day.

He was not used to a woman who appeared oblivious to the fact that he was male and she was female. No, nor one who stood toe-to-toe with him and refused to back down. He knew many tall women, models and actresses among others, but few who displayed such confidence and strength of mind.

He could hardly fault Guaio for leaping into her arms and wrapping himself around her. He would like to see for himself if she was as firm and yet womanly as she appeared.

Yes, and if, as a policewoman, she did it as politely as her shirt proclaimed.

What an imbecile he was to let such a thought distract him. He needed to be back in his Lamborghini, speeding down the road. The faster he cleared this traffic snarl, the sooner he could be gone.

Her small car was well out of the way, as she had shown the presence of mind not to venture too close to the stalled vehicles. With the cat Guaio lying across her shoulders, she retreated up the sloping road to stand beside it. Andrea nodded his approval as he slid into his car and reversed to within inches of her vehicle's front grill.

Out on the tarmac again, he spoke to the other drivers one by one, waving them back. He watched in amazement as they complied without argument. Scant minutes later, the Citroen that had been trapped against the rock face drove past Andrea with a typically rude gesture from the driver, one he returned with interest.

The larger delivery van was now free to complete the curve and pull over to make way for the bus. As the bus driver shifted gears, preparing to forge ahead toward Positano, Andrea turned away.

It was in that moment he saw the black sedan. It appeared at the top of the slope beyond the American's much smaller car, a dark, fog-shrouded shape that eased to a halt there with its engine thrumming.

Andrea plunged into a run, his gaze fastened on the woman with Guaio still wrapped around her neck. He shouted a warning, saw her turn toward him with her eyes widening in surprise.

The sedan rumbled to life and began to move. It gathered speed, heading straight toward the woman. She heard the sudden revving of the engine, for she swung her head in that direction.

Was the danger as clear to her as it seemed to him? It must have been, for she leaped away from her small car that sat almost against the rock guard wall, sprinting toward his Lamborghini. For an instant, Andrea thought she would be run down, but she slid into the open space on the far side of the heavy, low-slung vehicle.

The black sedan swerved to avoid the Lamborghini's back bumper, but skidded, fishtailing on the rain-slicked road. There was a dull thud and the shriek of metal on metal. An instant later, the sedan straightened and sped away, passing the line of cars and the bus that was just moving off before rounding the fog-shrouded curve on two wheels. Its engine roared as it was gunned, and then hummed away into the distance.

"*Signorina*! Are you all right? You are not hurt?" His voice rasped in his throat, the words harsh with strain. He reached with both hands to catch the American's forearms and draw her toward him from behind his car. His heart thudded against his ribs with such force he felt winded with it.

"I'm fine," she snapped. "But that crazy person hit my car!"

"It doesn't matter as long as you are safe." His relief was so great he hardly knew what he was saying.

"It may not matter to you, but it's a rental and I'll be liable for—"

She stopped with her lips parted and her eyes round with shock. Andrea turned his head to follow her gaze. He felt his own mouth fall open.

The nearest fender of her car was as crumpled and broken as cheap plastic. Yet that was not the worst of it. The force of the blow had slammed the light vehicle into the old stone wall that acted as a guard rail. The wall had broken apart, falling away down the cliff. Fully a third of the car's weight was now suspended over the edge, wavering up and down in thin air.

The woman at his side exclaimed and took a quick step toward the driver's side door.

"Wait!" Andrea shot out a hand to catch her arm, holding her in place.

She resisted only a second then was still. They stood transfixed as gravity increased the car's downward motion.

It reached the tipping point. Rock grated against metal as it began to slide.

The vehicle plunged over the edge, crashing down, tumbling with the clatter of breaking glass. Dull thuds sounded once, twice as it fell. A horrendous crash roared upward, echoing around them.

The sounds stopped.

Together, Andrea and the woman stepped to what was left of the stone barrier. The rental car lay below them, a ruined and crumpled heap on the rocks beside the sea.

Two

*T*he word that sprang to Dana's lips was profane but soul-satisfying. She usually avoided borrowing from the vocabulary of her male co-workers since it made her too much like them. But there were times when nothing else worked.

"*Certo*, for sure," the Italian beside her said with feeling.

His arm wrapped around her waist as if he felt she needed the support. Maybe she did. Her knees felt a little unhinged, though it was hard to say whether that was from watching everything she owned on this side of the ocean disappear or the heat and power of the Italian's body as it pressed against her hip and thigh.

It was hard to think. She was so far out of her comfort zone, much less her country and jurisdiction, that nothing made real sense.

"What should I do?" She moistened her dry lips. "I-I suppose I should notify the police."

"There is no time. We must go."

"Go? But I can't do that." She lifted a hand toward her face, and was startled to encounter the softness of fur. The cat was still firmly in place, its claws hooked into her T-shirt sleeve and its tail flicking back and forth in something less than feline calm.

"But we must."

"I have to report the accident. Then I need to call the rental company, maybe my insurance company and—and someone to bring up the car. But my cell phone is—is down there." She pulled her gaze away from the heap of metal at the base of the cliff, glanced up at the man who still held her. "I don't suppose—"

"You cannot stay here in the rain. Come with me and I will make these calls for you, explain everything to those you must contact."

She lifted a brow. "Will you, now?"

"All this will take time, much time. My home is not far away. It can be arranged, perhaps, for the police to come to you, also the rental agent. It will be convenient as they may require an interview with me at the same time."

"You?"

"I am a witness to what took place."

He was right on that point, still she frowned and shook her head. "That's very kind, but I don't know you. Frankly, I see no reason why you would bother."

"I am Andrea Tonello. And you are?"

Dana gave him her name with some reluctance. The rain had strengthened, and she was getting wetter by the second.

The cat around her neck was becoming agitated, too, more than likely disturbed by the rain as well as the strain in their voices.

What the Italian suggested made sense, and yet something seemed not quite right about it, something beyond the prospect of getting into a car with a strange man in a foreign country. Everything she'd ever read about women being kidnapped for sex trafficking crowded her brain until she felt a little sick with it.

"You will be quite safe, I assure you," Andrea Tonello said, his face serious. "My housekeeper will be there. She will make an espresso for us while we wait, or anything else you desire."

He was moving as he talked, urging her around to the passenger door of the Lamborghini. He glanced ahead toward the blind curve, as he opened it. His hand at her back was firm, almost pressing her inside, even as it sent shivers of awareness up and down her spine.

"Where I come from, it's a crime to leave the scene of an accident," she said, resisting the final step that would take her inside the car.

"This is hardly the same thing. Please believe me when I say all will be well."

"You'll see to it, I suppose."

"Just as you say," he agreed.

There was such smooth assurance in his voice she almost believed him, might have if he had not been so determined to take her away. "I can't let you do that, really," she said as she unwound her feline neck warmer. "Here, take your cat. If you'll just make that call to the police for me, I'll stay here until everything is settled."

He made no move to accept Guaio. Instead, he tipped his head as if listening as he turned his gaze back toward the curve ahead. Dana grew aware of the low roar of an oncoming engine.

"*Mi dispiace*, I am sorry."

Abruptly, she was half lifted, half shoved into the vehicle. The door slammed behind her.

Dana landed on her shoulder with a squalling, indignant cat in her face. By the time she shoved upright, disentangled her T-shirt from the cat's sharp claws and faced forward, Andrea had flung into the driver's seat. He fired the Lamborghini into a powerful, grumbling readiness. Shoving it into gear, he skimmed out of the line of traffic.

The vehicle accelerated with dizzying leaps of speed that pressed her back into the passenger seat. They flew past one car, two, and then skidded around the curve on the back bumper of the tourist bus that had been first in line. Speeding out of the turn, they surged ahead of the bus and onto a straightaway.

Coming toward them at break-neck speed was a black sedan with the forms of two men inside. Dana, clinging to the dash with both hands, whipped her head around as it sped past. She recognized the shattered headlamp that was a souvenir of the impact that had pushed her rental over the cliff.

"That's the car that hit mine!" she cried, swinging toward the man beside her. "The driver must be coming back to see about the accident."

"He's coming back for something," he said, his gaze flicking toward his rear view mirror for an instant.

"We have to go back."

"Do we, indeed? Even if hitting your car was no accident?"

She stared at him while the air left her lungs. "What are you saying? Why would that happen? I don't know a single soul in Italy except the friends I'm supposed to meet."

His face turned grim. "You know me now. Or it may look as if you do. You know Guaio."

"What does that mean?" She glanced at the cat that had wound up in the area behind the front seats as she paused for an answer. When he made none, she took a deep breath, let it out in a rush. "Look, I don't know what's going on here, but I want no part of it. If you'll just take me to a police station—"

"I can't do that."

"Why in hell not?"

She'd been as patient as she knew how to be, but this was too much. It didn't matter if he was as handsome as Apollo himself; she wasn't ready to die with him when his Lamborghini took a flying leap off this winding excuse for a highway as her poor little rental car had done.

"No time," he answered, and veered off the road onto a half hidden driveway without slackening speed an iota.

Vines and tree limbs whipped past so close Dana ducked instinctively. The road twisted and turned, snaking ever upward. Andrea worked the stick shift, his movements smooth and perfectly coordinated as he took switchbacks as if they were no more taxing than a Sunday drive.

Dana did not want to admire that ease and expertise, yet it was impossible to ignore it. She'd taken driver's courses, knew how difficult it was to maintain control under these conditions. That didn't make her mind any easier.

"Where are we going?" she demanded with her voice as even as she could make it. "And what are you going to do? I'd like answers, and I'd like them now."

He gave her the merest flash of his green eyes. "We are going to my home, as I said before. Once there, I will call the police, also as I said before."

Why did she not believe him?

She should, no doubt. He didn't appear to be a criminal type. His car shouted money. His jeans might be comfortably worn but had started life in some designer's atelier. She wouldn't be surprised if his shoes had been handmade. His hair had been trimmed by an expert, and he wore a ring on the middle finger of his right hand that had the look of 24-karat antique gold and carried the *bas relief* of a sailing ship. His manner was upper class with the distinct whiff of tasteful wealth.

Yet something about his manner swung the needle on her professional crap detector.

It was a crying shame, it really was. Suzanne and Caryn had laughed and joked about finding Italian heartthrobs on the Amalfi Coast, one for each of them. They'd toasted the idea in champagne on the night before the other two left Atlanta. Her friends would have loved meeting Andrea if only to look at him in all his Oh-My-God handsome, macho Italian perfection.

Italian heartthrob indeed.

Well, all right. Maybe it was possible. Maybe she was wrong. Andrea could be the genuine article and she was being suspicious for nothing. She would wait and see. But heaven help the man if he tried anything.

Dana reached for the cat that was trying to creep into her lap from the back of the Lamborghini. She wrapped her arms around the soft and comforting warmth of his body, holding him against her.

Animals had always responded to her for some reason. Her brothers swore it was because she identified with them and had no fear, though she didn't buy that entirely. Still it seemed a good sign that Guaio not only allowed her to hold him close, but reached to rub his face along her chin.

The house, or rather the mansion, appeared ahead of them as the long driveway-like road ended. Like an eagle's nest high on a green plateau, it overlooked the wide, endless vista of the sea above the surrounding treetops. It was modern in style, with sweeping lines, acres of glass, and a serene lack of interest in making an impression. If there was a pool, tennis court, putting green or any of the other trappings of an indolent lifestyle, they were not evident. The only sign of anything out of the ordinary was the helipad below the house and the sleek black and silver helicopter that squatted upon it.

The view of the house was perfectly clear, she realized after a moment. Raindrops were no longer speckling the windshield. The fog had lifted as well, or else they had driven above it. Even as she noticed, Andrea reached to flick the wipers to their off position.

Iron gates opened at the touch of a transmitter to allow entry to the estate. Substantial but simple in style, they closed behind them. Twisting to watch them, Dana felt an unpleasant sense of being confined.

"How long do you suppose this will take?" she asked as she faced forward again. "I have friends expecting me."

"Do you? Where is this?"

She told him, glad of the excuse to make it clear she would be missed if she didn't turn up.

He did not look at her as he sent the car along a circular drive. "You should call them, I expect. It may be several hours before everything is settled."

"My cell was in my purse, and my purse in the car, if you'll remember."

"*Certo*," he said in laconic reply. "You are free to use my phone to call anyone you wish, though the signal is better inside the house." He paused. "I would guess all else of value was in this purse? Your wallet, passport and return air ticket, perhaps?"

"Good guess." As hard as it was to believe, everything she had, including every stitch of clothing she had packed for the trip, was at the bottom of that cliff. All she had was what she was wearing. "You think they will be able to recover anything?"

He eased to a stop where the drive widened into a small court before the mansion's front entrance. "Let us hope. It will not be easy, as you may imagine, so could take considerable time."

"How much time is 'considerable'?"

"A day or two, perhaps more. Who can say?"

She had no patience with such an easy-going attitude, not when it was her personal belongings scattered over rocks several feet down a sheer cliff. "The towing company should be able to make a guess."

"But they can't begin until the police investigation is complete."

"What is there to investigate? My rental was side-swiped and went through the barrier. That's all there is to it."

"Except that it happened while someone was trying to run you down."

"You don't know that!"

It wasn't something Dana wanted to think about, mainly because it made no sense. No one knew who she was or had any idea she would be at that particular place at that time. And yet it had seemed the car aimed straight for her and poor Guaio. The cat had thought so, too, judging from the claw marks she could feel gouged into one shoulder.

"I know what I saw," Andrea answered as he swung open the door and got out.

It was an instant before she realized he was moving around to get her door. All manners aside, the last thing she needed was to have to put her hand in his or touch him in any way; physical contact was far too disturbing. She shoved her own door open and slid out, rising to her feet with Guaio held against her.

Andrea's shrug was so small she might have missed it if she had not been expecting it. Still, he indicated with a polite gesture that she should precede him up the wide stone steps that led to the front entrance.

It opened as they approached. A short, rotund woman with graying hair and a sweet smile stepped back to allow them to enter. Andrea spoke to her in rapid Italian before turning to Dana.

"I have asked Maria, the housekeeper I mentioned, to show you upstairs and find something dry for you to wear so you may be more comfortable. Come down when you are ready. I'll make the necessary phone calls, and then join you in the sitting room over there."

Dana glanced toward the room he indicated, an enormous, light-filled expanse on the front of the house with a bountiful sea view and at least four different conversational groupings done in shades of gray-blue and ochre. At least she should have no trouble finding such a huge room again, Dana thought. She nodded her understanding before turning to follow the housekeeper.

The shirt Maria found her was a rust-red polo. Maria appeared to consider the color a nice foil for the auburn of Dana's hair, judging from her smile and gentle tug on her ponytail. Dana refused the offer of more as her jeans and sneakers were damp but not really wet. She was happy to be left alone with the shirt, even if she did feel just a bit deserted as Guaio struggled out of her arms and followed the housekeeper from the room.

The bedroom to which she had been shown was

apparently designed for guests, being elegantly upscale but with nothing personal about it. She availed herself of the connecting bath, hardly pausing for proper appreciation of its marble fittings, mirrored walls and other amenities. She did remove the band that held her hair and finger comb the wayward strands, but that was it. The sooner she was out of Andrea Tonello's home and on her way again, the better she would like it.

She winced as she pulled off her T-shirt. It had stuck to the claw marks on her shoulder. They began bleeding again as she pulled the fabric away. She washed them as well as she could, and then pressed her damp shirt to them. At least the rust-red of the shirt she'd been given would help disguise any blood spots.

The polo shirt, when she pulled it on, looked like a sleep shirt on her. Obviously borrowed from her host's closet, the sleeves came to her elbows and the hem struck her well below her hips. It was incredibly soft, however, and beautifully made with no sign whatever of a manufacturer's tag or designer's logo.

It did have a personal identification tag.

Whoever heard of having knit polo shirts made to order? Dana, spreading the tail of it as she turned this way and that in front of a full-length mirror, shook her head. If anything more was required to let her know she was out of her league with Andrea Tonello, this was it.

He had changed also; she saw that at once as she entered the sitting room. Gone was the cream sweater he'd worn earlier. In its place was a shirt in clear green that fit without a single wrinkle. He stood relaxed at the window, staring out at the watery sunlight brought by the clearing weather. He held a small cup of espresso in one hand while the other was shoved into the pocket of a pair of gray slacks in a way that drew attention to the rear view.

Dana felt her heart trip in her chest.

Yes, the sooner she was away from Andrea Tonello, the better.

"You spoke to the police?" she asked, keeping her voice steady with an effort.

"*Si.* I did, yes." He turned to face her, a smile lighting his eyes before he moved toward a coffee service that sat on a low table made of some exotic wood. "Will you have an espresso or *caffè e latte*?"

She recognized that choice from her favorite Italian restaurant menu. "With milk, if you please. I've never acquired a taste for espresso."

"Stay in Italy long enough and it will come," he said easily. He set his cup aside, took a silver pot in each hand and filled a cup with streams of hot coffee and hot milk. The cat Guaio, sitting on a cushion on a nearby sofa, stopped his grooming to watch the operation with narrow-eyed interest.

"I doubt there will be time," she said, her smile a little wry as she took the cup he handed her. The coffee was perfect. Feeling its reviving heat, she realized how chilled she'd become. No doubt a part of it was the shock of nearly being run over, as well as watching her belongings vanish before her eyes.

"Only a short holiday then?"

"The usual two weeks."

"Not nearly long enough. You should have a month, at least."

"I wish." She went on to tell him about Suzanne and Caryn, and the house they had rented.

"Perhaps you will come again next year, since you have found your way," he said courteously when she had finished.

She met his gaze for an instant. The green of his shirt did sinful things for the color of his eyes, not that she had any interest in that rather disturbing phenomenon. "Yes, perhaps."

"Excellent."

Enough polite chit-chat, she thought. It was time this show got on the road. "So what did the police say? Is it okay that we left the scene of the accident, or should I go back? Will I be all right even if unable to produce my passport or International driver's permit for identification?"

"We did not get into the details, but please, you must not worry so much. All will be well."

Was that possible? She didn't know, and that was the problem. "Surely they want to talk to me?"

He drained his cup then studied the golden brown stain left inside by the strong brew. "They do, yes."

"You mentioned before that they might come here. Is that the plan?"

"Unfortunately, that isn't convenient at this time. They request that you present yourself at the police station in Positano."

Was that normal? It must not be since Andrea seemed a little uneasy. She was on edge herself, though officialdom usually held no terrors for her. It was good to know they were about to set the accident investigation in motion.

"I'm fine with that," she said firmly. "If everything is straightened out in time, maybe they will be able to bring up the rental car this afternoon."

"And you can then be on your way to your friends."

She gave him a relieved smile. "Exactly."

"*Bene*," he said. "We will take the helicopter."

Dana had just swallowed the last of her coffee. She choked, coughed to clear her throat. Her voice had a strangled sound when she was finally able to speak. "The helicopter! But why, what's wrong with the car?"

A pained expression crossed his face. "I thought you wanted speed."

"I'd say that Lamborghini of yours has more than enough."

"But in the chopper we will not be confined to the coast road, need not make every curve or worry about trailing along behind a tourist bus or some government worker who wishes to arrive home in time for lunch but not a minute before. It is a practical matter, you see?"

She saw, all right, but she still didn't like it.

How had it come to this she wondered in despair? What had happened to her carefully planned vacation?

By now, she should have been in Positano with Suzanne and Caryn, sipping wine and comparing travel stories. Instead, she was here in a strange house with a strange man, about to take off in a helicopter to face a police inquiry in a language she didn't understand.

It could be the police spoke English, of course. They must be used to tourists from Canada, Australia and the UK, as well as Americans. Somehow the possibility did not reassure her.

"You will be on hand to translate?" she asked. "I know it's an imposition, but—"

"Yes, naturally I will be there as they wish also to speak to me."

No doubt they did. He was a witness, as he'd pointed out before. She pressed her lips together and breathed deep through her nose. "Fine, then. But before we go, I should call my friends to let them know I'll be delayed."

He snapped his fingers and reached to take his cell phone from his pants pocket. "But of course, I had forgotten. They must not be allowed to worry."

The call went to voice mail.

For the sake of economy, Suzanne and Caryn had only one cell phone between them. Whether they had it turned off or left it behind in the room while they went out was not possible to guess. Dana left a brief message to say she'd run into a problem and would be late arriving. She didn't want to alarm them too much, so the details could wait. Besides, she hoped to be with them before the day was done.

"They did not answer?" Andrea asked as she ended the call.

She passed the cell to him with a small shake of her head. "I'll call again from the police station, if you don't mind. Suzanne and Caryn may be able to meet me there when we're done."

"A good plan. And so?"

She met his gaze, her own clear and full of purpose. "So when do we leave?"

His smile was something more than approving. "Now, *cara mia*. We go at once."

Had he called her his dear in that heart-stopping accent of his? The question distracted her as they left the house and walked across the lawn toward the helipad. Well what if he had? As with her grandmother's friends in Atlanta who called everyone honey or sugar, it most likely meant nothing.

Guaio slipped out of the house behind them, winding around Dana's ankles, running ahead and then looking back to be sure they were coming. Dana hated to disappoint the cat, but could see no help for it. He could hardly go to the police station.

Andrea glanced at the seal point, but did nothing to stop him from following. No doubt he knew the noise of the helicopter would send him racing back to the house, Dana thought. There was no need to worry.

The helicopter was as sleek in its way as Andrea's Lamborghini, and also larger than it had appeared from the driveway. There was no sign of a pilot anywhere around, but Andrea did not hesitate. He swung open the side door, waited for the power steps to slide out and helped Dana inside.

She was faced with five seats, all in gray leather.

Choosing the nearest, she dropped down into it. She was still rubbing her elbow to soothe the tingle where Andrea had grasped it when her Italian host scooped up Guaio, bounded up to the steps and set the tom cat on her lap.

"Well, looks as if you get to go, after all," she murmured as she reached automatically to grasp the warm and furry body. "I can't wait to see who babysits you while we're at the police station."

If Andrea heard, he gave no sign. Closing and latching the door behind him, he made his way to the pilot's seat.

She should have known. It made perfect sense that piloting himself would be faster and more convenient.

"You could come up here, if you like," he called back to her. "The view will be much better."

No doubt it would. The prospect of that wider view warred with caution inside her, however. "Maybe I should stay here and hold Guaio."

"I transferred his carrier from my car, and it's now between the seats directly behind you. It will be best if he travels in it."

The man had an answer for everything. It could become irritating if she let it.

The cat seemed willing enough to be put into the carrier. That argued he was used to it. Could be she needed to adjust her thinking to allow for a rich and possibly eccentric Italian who thought nothing of carrying a cat with him everywhere he went.

The engine was humming and the rotors turning, beginning to whine, by the time she took the copilot's seat.

Andrea handed her a helmet with built-in headphones, reaching to tuck a strand of her hair out of the way as he fitted it on her head.

She controlled a shiver at that brief touch. It meant nothing to him, or so it seemed, but she was not used to such casual intimacies.

If he noticed her reaction, he gave no sign. His smile as he met her eyes was probably meant to be encouraging but had the opposite effect. If this was such a common, everyday method of travel, why would she need reassurance?

Moments later, they lifted off the ground, rocking a little as they rose above the encroaching trees, the bulk of the house and mountain slope behind it. The helicopter swooped forward, banked and made a wide turn, heading out along the coast. It hummed along at terrific speed, zipping over the miles. Andrea Tonello had been right about the time savings in this mode of travel.

"You are all right?"

Dana dragged her gaze from the ribbon of winding, looping, vehicle-studded roadway below as she realized Andrea was talking to her through the helmet's earphones. For the past several minutes, he had been exchanging comments in staccato Italian with some kind of air traffic control somewhere.

"I'm great," she said, giving him a quick thumb's up. She was, too. It was good to be on her way to Positano again. The smoothness of the flight, also the easy and familiar way Andrea handled controls, watching the array of dials and gauges, inspired nothing but confidence.

"*Va bene.* It will not be a long journey, this I promise you."

She didn't mind how long it was, or she wouldn't if she wasn't so worried about her belongings that might be washing out to sea at that very moment. Excitement bubbled in her veins as she gazed around, fascinated by the distant gray-blue shapes of the hills, the rocky landscape directly below and glorious blue-green of the Mediterranean sea.

She couldn't wait to see Suzanne and Caryn and tell them about this wild adventure. They weren't going to believe it, never in a million years. She wasn't sure she believed it herself.

It was just as well everyone in the States didn't know what was going on at this moment, she thought. Her mom and dad and two brothers worried enough about her being a cop; she was the baby of the family, after all. While the whole bunch would be fit to be tied if they found out everything she owned was at the bottom of a cliff, her brothers would be especially horrified. They could short-sheet her bed, superglue her doll's clothes to its body and dye her kitten's hair pink, but no one else had better mess with her.

Turning in her seat, she looked back to check on Guaio. The cat deliberately turned his stare away, as if bored or else annoyed at being shut up. Otherwise, he was okay in his rather palatial carrier that was lined with blue velvet and had stainless steel water and food bowls attached to the gridded door. She faced forward again.

"You like cats," Andrea said with a slight tilt to his smile.

"How did you guess?" Her laugh was self-deprecating. "I

have two at home, though neither with Guaio's bloodlines."

"Not many are so rare. He is a champion in his class, as my sister would be the first to tell you."

"Your sister?"

"He belongs to her, you realize."

"I see. And he's a show cat?" It made sense. Guaio had that form and presence, also that kind of intense grooming.

"She was involved in showing him at one time, but not anymore."

"The competition is fierce, I believe, not to mention expensive."

"It wasn't that, so much as—well, other things intervened."

"And now you have him."

Andrea gave her a glance tinged with irony. "A temporary arrangement. At least, I trust so."

"I can't imagine why. He seems perfectly well-behaved."

"You haven't been around him long or you would never say that."

"Yet you take him wherever you go." Skepticism was in her smile as she met his green gaze. "I think you like him, but just don't want to admit it."

"You are deluded," he answered, though his well-formed mouth twitched at one corner.

"I'll bet his name isn't Guaio, either. What is it really? Something noble and a half-mile long?"

"A full mile, at least. It is Petrarca Vittorio Galilei Justinius Machiavelli III."

Just listening to the syllables roll off Andrea's tongue in

deep, rounded tones was enough to bring a woman with less self-control to near orgasm. Dana smoothed the hair on her arm back down from its prickly, upstanding position. "Machiavelli, the authority on princely conniving? You're making that up!"

He gave a low chuckle. "Yes, I confess, though the rest is quite legitimate. And you may discover there is some accuracy in my addition."

He was devastating in this mood. He really was, darn the man. It was a good thing they would be at the police station soon, and she could put all this behind her.

Dana glanced forward to check out their progress. She blinked then turned to stare out the tinted window beside her. A soft exclamation left her.

There was nothing around them except water. While they were talking, they had left the coast behind. The helicopter was now flying out over the empty Mediterranean.

"Is this a more direct route than following the coast road?" she asked in clipped concern.

"You could say so."

She swung to stare at him with a frown between her brows. "No. I want you to say so."

He didn't answer, but only reached to adjust a switch on the panel in front of him.

Dana watched him in some perplexity. What did she know of air traffic patterns in this area, after all? Nothing. He could be following any set of coordinates and she'd never know. Yet why hadn't he explained? He could have said something, even if he thought she wouldn't understand.

His silence seemed to mean only one thing. She could feel the increasing beat of her heart, sense the release of stress hormones like poison in her bloodstream. She swallowed before bringing out the question that rolled like thunder in her brain.

"Where are we going?"

He gave her a brief look before facing forward again. "Somewhere you will be safe."

"I'd feel pretty safe at the police station."

"You can't stay there forever."

She took a deep breath while clinging hard to the remnants of her composure. "Correct me if I'm wrong, but I was fine until I met you."

"You were."

"What is it I'm supposed to be kept safe from now? Who were the men in the car that hit mine, and why did they do that? Who are you that I'm suddenly in danger because I'm close to you?"

"It isn't me."

Oh, please. If it isn't you, I suppose it's Guaio. He's the one who's so dangerous."

"He isn't dangerous, but—" He stopped, shook his head. "I'll tell you all about it when we land. Until then, it will be best if you sit back, relax, and let me get us there without incident."

"Relax? You want me to relax when you're virtually kidnapping me?" She could hear her voice rising, but couldn't do a thing about it.

"The pertinent word is *virtually*. You came of your own free will."

She crossed her arms over her breast, clasping her arms tightly on either side. "That was because I thought I knew where we were going. Now I don't. Just where is *there*, if it isn't too much to ask?"

"An island."

"An island," she repeated blankly.

"A private island. *Isola delle Palme delle Tonellos.*"

"Delle Tonellos? Does that mean—"

"It belongs to my family, has for generations."

His own island. Wasn't that nice? Private, too. And isolated no doubt. Also not easy to get to if he needed a helicopter for the trip.

This couldn't be happening. She felt cold inside, afraid to believe it could turn out all right, afraid to think it wouldn't. "What's so great about going there? What makes it safer for me than anywhere else?"

"It is an island," he reiterated. The glance he sent her was less than patient.

"Meaning?"

"No one can land on it without someone knowing. Security is more certain."

"More certain than the police." The scathing sound of the words underlined her disbelief.

"In this case, yes."

"And from what, exactly, do I need to be secure?"

"It is a family matter, one too complicated to go into just now."

She sat unmoving, watching lacy white caps that topped the blue waves passing rapidly beneath them, also the small, moving shadow of the helicopter cast upon them. When she spoke again, her lips were so stiff it was difficult to form the words.

"You never called the police, did you?"

THREE

"*I* reported the accident."

Andrea chose those words with such care that it was he who felt Machiavellian. His intentions were the best, but Dana Marsden was unlikely to believe that at this moment.

She was amazingly calm, given the circumstances. Most women would be screaming, shouting at him, demanding he turn around and set them down in Positano. That she was not made him distinctly wary.

People resorted to screaming and shouting when they felt helpless. This American policewoman with her amazing Titian red hair shining in the sun through the cockpit window could well have other responses in mind. It put him on his guard.

"But you did not tell the police you knew where I was," she said with fury leaping like fire in the golden brown of her eyes.

"On the contrary. I said you were safe and taking shelter from the rain."

"It isn't raining now. They will expect me to show up."

He lifted a shoulder, his gaze on the blue land mass coming up on the horizon just where it should be. "Not at the police station."

"No. Of course not. I should have known."

"They will not assume you are missing, and that is the main thing."

"For now, but what about later?"

"Later we shall see."

She gave him a hard stare. The faintest of tremors sounded in her voice when she spoke, but it still held deadly promise in its quiet cadence. "I don't know what you think you're doing, but I can tell you this much. I will press charges against you for kidnapping if I ever do see a police station."

Andrea adjusted the controls, felt the helicopter begin its gradual descent toward the speck of green and brown in the blue water ahead. "Children are kidnapped. You, *cara*, have been abducted."

"Don't call me that," she snapped. "I am not your dear."

"Perhaps not." Though he did not speak the words, his tone said, *and perhaps so, in time.*

Her eyes narrowed. "Whether it's kidnapped or abducted, I suspect the police will have the correct word when they arrest you."

She had courage. He would grant her that. "First, of course, they will have to be convinced there was a crime that requires an arrest."

"What do you mean?"

"As far as they know, the damage to your car was purest accident. Now you are enjoying an unexpected holiday and will reclaim your belongings when you tire of being my companion. My man of business has been instructed to arrange the retrieval of the rental vehicle at my expense, and to see everything in it is kept safe."

"Your companion!"

He gave her a wry glance. "It's not unknown for a woman to be seen with me."

"I'm sure. And you think you can get away with this because you're some hotshot, mega-rich Italian playboy."

"I am no playboy at all, but *si, cara*, I do think so. I think it because I have done so already."

He thought she was going to hit him, as he saw her hands clench into fists, and tensed for the blow. Not that he blamed her. She had a right to be doubtful of his intentions, as well as furious at how he had tricked her.

Self-preservation seemed to trump rage, however. She glanced at the helipad fast coming toward them and turned to stare out the window again.

Such control was admirable in its way, yet a challenge to any red-blooded Italian male. What might it take to destroy it, he wondered? How would she look with her face flushed, her lips soft and moist instead of clamped together, and her eyes heated with something other than righteous rage?

He needed to get his mind back on what he was doing before he overshot the helipad. This was a protective, humanitarian abduction, not a prelude to seduction. He had no business fastening his gaze on Dana Marsden lips or thinking about how she might look with that glorious hair spread over his pillow. Or *Dio guardi*, over his chest.

The nicely rounded shapes of her breasts under the shirt he had loaned her were off limits, as were the slender lengths of her legs in her figure-molding jeans. To try picturing how she might look in something more feminine and stylish was of no use whatever.

Or was it? Her belongings, including the clothing she must have brought with her to Italy, were at the bottom of the cliff. It was possible he could work with that. What woman did not enjoy attractive, well-made designer fashions?

It would be best if he soothed Dana's ire and persuaded her to accept her isolation with him over the next few hours or even days. Matters would be far too uncomfortable otherwise. And if the prospect was something he was beginning to anticipate, that was his reward for getting mixed up in this crazy business in the first place.

The landing on the island was not the smoothest he'd ever made. No matter, it was done.

Relief sang along Andrea's veins, mingling with the inescapable rush of testosterone brought by his inconvenient fantasies. It would be best if he curbed both. The island was as close to a refuge as he could come on short notice, but it was not completely safe. He would do well to strengthen his self-control to match that of his guest.

He had never considered the villa and surrounding land,

with its gray-green olive groves, palm and scrub forest and meadowland covered with herbs and wildflowers, in the light of a fortress. He did so now as he stepped out of the helicopter. The villa appeared rather like a small village, being a series of connected cubes that meandered along the slope of this highest point on the island. Its walls were nearly two feet thick, built to withstand the storms that swirled up from the depths of the surrounding sea or the wild and dusty *sirocco* winds that blew in from Africa. That these same thick walls had made life inside them bearable in the days before such amenities as electricity or air conditioning was also a part of its history.

It had been renovated in the 1960s by his grandfather for the sake of jet-set guests and the occasional actress of international fame. The old man had installed larger windows, added a few more balconies and a stepped terrace leading to an Olympic-sized pool.

Andrea's father had done little more than provide upkeep, as he had no use for either society or progress. Or perhaps there had not been time as he had died only a scant few years after Andrea's grandfather.

The helipad was Andrea's contribution. That was in addition to having the place redecorated to suit his personal inclinations and its more rugged past.

The front door was massive and would be easily guarded. The only back entrance was from the kitchen area, and the heavy door there was still fitted with an ancient iron latch closed by a stout steel bar. The weakest point of the villa seemed the terrace with its series of glass-paned doors that opened into the living room, study and master bedroom. Well, and perhaps the balconies attached to some of the guest rooms.

An ear-numbing yowl routed all thought. Guaio was apparently tired of being confined and ignored. Wincing a little, Andrea reached inside for the cat's carrier and then jolted down the last of the chopper's steps. He joined Dana who had exited first and now stood well beyond the rotors that were winding to a stop.

She had made no attempt to run. He was glad to see she recognized the futility of it.

"So you own all this," she said with a flip of one hand toward the land that sloped down to the sea. Her lips curled at one corner. "Must be nice."

"Pleasant, yes," he answered, his voice mild. He tipped his head toward the villa. "Shall we?"

"I suppose you bought the island as some kind of bachelor retreat."

"Not at all. My family settled here more than six hundred years ago. They claimed it without cost, but have paid for every inch many times over as they fought to hold it."

"They sound like pirates."

"Fishermen, rather, when they weren't defending the place. Though I imagine they scavenged what they could when a ship foundered at their doorstep." His smile was sardonic as he noted the way she walked along beside him, so intent on insulting him she required no coercion. It could also be she was intelligent enough to see there was little alternative.

She made a sound that could have been a laugh or a soft snort. "You aren't going to tell me fishing made you what you are today."

"By no means. One of my ancestors started building ships, and discovered a few secrets in the process that he turned into money. Since then we've all just added to it."

"So whatever you have comes from simple industry."

Her scathing glance took in the villa, the island, the helicopter and even the rather ridiculous carrier his sister had bought for Guaio. Andrea resented her tone, but that did not prevent him from noticing the way sunlight turned her hair to flame and highlighted the clarity of her skin. No, nor how his shirt hugged her breasts and skimmed the outline of her hips. He took a discreet breath before he answered.

"With the addition of a few investments, some wise, some lucky, nearly all profitable."

"But not criminal. That part, you seem to have inaugurated all on your own."

The back of his neck prickled with the sudden heat of anger. He stopped, turned to face her. "I am not a criminal. Since we are here now, I will tell you why it was necessary to remove you from the place where we met and the incident that brought us together. When I am done, you may call me what you like, but I believe you will realize I could not have acted in any other way, not and live with the consequences."

"Fine. Spit it out," she answered, facing him with her fists on her hips. "What is this great mystery? I'm dying to hear why you are so sure the only way to keep me safe, as you call it, is to make me your prisoner."

Guaio squalled again, an unearthly shriek followed by growls and grumbles. Andrea could almost have sworn the cat was in sympathy with Dana as he was also a prisoner.

"Soon," he said above the cat's noise. "For now, I must see to Guaio and make certain the staff received the message about your arrival."

There was irony in the last for it was clear Maria, his housekeeper from the mainland, had alerted her cousin Luisa who held the same position at the villa. It would be an unusual development in their eyes, as he did not, as a rule, bring women to the island. No, no matter what he might have led Dana to believe.

Luisa, along with her great-nephew Tommaso and two older cousins who worked as gardeners, would be concerned for their positions. This, though their families had worked for his for generations, coming in daily and returning home at night. He must remember to let them know the arrival of his guest did not mean they were about to have a new mistress.

One of Dana's red-gold brows went up as she saw the cluster of people waiting at the front entrance. He thought she also relaxed a bit, perhaps at the realization she would not be completely alone with him. In any case, she was pleasant enough if a little stiff, shaking hands in the American fashion as he introduced each staff member.

Andrea spoke briefly to his housekeeper before turning to his guest to translate. "Luisa will show you to your room. Lunch will be served on the terrace when you have had a chance to settle in, perhaps relax a bit. We will talk there."

The look Dana gave him should have shriveled him to the size of a garden gnome. Andrea was made of sterner stuff. He smiled into the hot brown depths of her eyes as he bowed her into his island home.

~ ~ ~

The nerve of the man was beyond belief. That he would simply fly off with her to this out-of-the-way place did not seem real. It was even more incredible that he thought he could do whatever he pleased and get away with it. Anger sizzled through her veins like acid at the very idea.

He was mistaken. It would be a pleasure to convince him of it.

Yes, but how? What was she going to do?

It might help her decide if she knew what was behind this ridiculous abduction. It apparently had something to do with the black car that had almost hit her back on the coast road.

Did Andrea know who was in it? Was there some connection between them?

Was he some kind of Mafioso kingpin with his Lamborghini, private helicopter and multiple houses?

The need to know the answers to these questions was nearly as white-hot as the fury inside her. Curiosity had always been one of her be-setting faults. She'd joined the police, in part, because she always wanted to figure out who the bad guy was and why he committed his crimes. Not that she'd had much chance of it yet; as a mere traffic cop, she was a long way from making detective.

She would learn more at lunch, or at least hear whatever explanation her Italian host trotted out for her. It might or might not be the truth. She would have to decide whether it was or wasn't when she heard it. Then she would see.

Meanwhile, it appeared she was to be treated as a guest rather than a prisoner. It was as well. She did not take well to confinement.

As abductions went, this one was courteous enough, she had to concede. She hadn't been threatened, coerced or manhandled in any way. Well, except for being shoved into a car when she balked. She should be thankful for that much at least.

Being duped ticked her off, nonetheless. It wasn't something she was going to forgive and forget, no matter what Andrea Tonello had to say about it.

Dana liked the island villa better than Andrea's modern house they'd left behind earlier. Though there seemed scant rhyme or reason in its arrangement on different levels, nearly every room commanded a stupendous sea view, as well as overlooking the front lawn with its helipad off to one side.

The other house had seemed sterile, almost hermetically sealed away from life, love and the possibility of human interaction. The interior of this island villa, with its high ceilings, odd wall angles and short runs of marble steps between floors, was the exact opposite. It held the feeling of having grown organically with much living enjoyed within its ancient walls.

Its windows and doors stood open so curtains of fine

white linen lifted and billowed in the sea breeze that brought the scents of brine, flowers and sun-warmed herbs. There was a comfortable lack of pretense in its worn rugs that were yet priceless, the soft, well-plumped pillows on the overstuff sofas that invited naps, mosaics on the walls that would be impervious to damage from children or animals, and frescos with all-too-human gods and goddesses staring down, some with lascivious glints in their eyes. It was a lived-in house and the better for it.

Dana breathed deep, trying to identify the herbs that scented the air. Thyme? Rosemary? Oregano? She wasn't sure, but thought it might be all three. She could get used to it, whatever the combination. It would be a shame, she thought, if there was nothing like it near the house Caryn and Suzanne had rented.

Turning away from the window where she'd been gazing out to sea, she glanced at the bed that was centered in the room. It was fairly high off the floor, no doubt for air circulation, and covered in a combination of white and pale green bed linens that were piled with pillows of all shapes and sizes. It appeared amazingly sleep-worthy, and she stifled a yawn brought on by just looking at it.

She was tired, and no wonder; it must have been at least thirty hours since she'd slept, as she'd left home the day before, flown all night, laid over in Rome before changing planes for Naples and then picked up her rental at the airport and headed at once for Positano. With just a little encouragement, she could crawl into the middle of that bed and sleep for hours.

It wouldn't do. The last thing she needed was to get too comfortable here.

An island in the Mediterranean. How on earth was she to get away from it?

Dana looked for a phone but there was none. It didn't greatly surprise her as most of her friends relied on their cell phones these days. She must remember to borrow Andrea's phone again to contact Caryn and Suzanne.

Yes, but would he hand it over as he had before? She would have to try it and see.

She left the room a few minutes later, going quickly down the stairs and making her way toward the terrace that lay at one end of the house. Emerging upon that open, flagstone paved area, she glanced around. A table under a vine covered pergola was set for lunch, but neither Andrea nor anyone else was in sight.

The angle of the terrace, as with so much of the house, gave a view of the front lawn. Her attention was drawn to its sunny emptiness, also to the helipad that lay just beyond its gray-green expanse.

The helicopter sat there a mere couple of hundred feet away, looking like a giant silver and black dragonfly. It seemed to draw her like a magnet.

She made no decision, hatched no particular plan. She simply walked down the terrace steps, and kept right on walking until she was close enough to touch the chopper that had brought her to Andrea's island and might, with a little luck, take her away again. Try as she might, she couldn't remember it being locked after they landed. She reached for the door handle.

The distinct metallic click of a lock engaging stopped her. She lowered her hand, stood still for an instant before turning slowly to face the villa.

Andrea stood in the terrace doorway with one shoulder propped on its frame. He lifted a hand to give her a small salute. In it was what appeared to be the remote key control for the helicopter.

To actually try the door of the helicopter would be futile. Dana swung into movement, marching toward where Andrea stepped out onto the terrace to wait for her. And with each and every stride, she damned him using every swearword she'd ever heard in her three years on the police force.

"I poured a *limoncello* for you," he said as she came close enough to hear. "It seemed you might not have tried our famous liqueur as you just arrived in Italy."

Andrea had slipped the remote into his pants pocket by the time she reached him, so removing the reminder of how easily she had been foiled. His voice was casual, without a trace of gloating. As difficult as it might be, matching his civility as if nothing had happened seemed a better option than pitching an undignified fit. Her answer was blunt and ungracious, then, but not as sulky as she felt.

"No, I haven't."

"You should enjoy it if you like the taste of lemons."

He turned to walk with her along the edge of the flagstone area which stepped down in wide levels that diminished in width until they became steps that continued down to the sea. She glanced at him, then away again. She could be as blasé as he was if she put her mind to it. And she would if it killed her.

"So it's Italian lemonade?"

"You might call it that. It is a favorite here in Italy's Amalfitano region, and made all along the coast. The zest of Femminello St. Teresa lemons is the main ingredient, of course, though it is steeped in alcohol and mixed with sugar syrup."

"Alcohol?"

The glance he sent her was amused. "Of course, though not too strong. I will admit it is usually served after dinner, but it seemed beneficial to have it now. Lunch will be delayed some few minutes as Louisa had only short notice of our arrival."

The liqueur was set out on the glass topped table she'd noticed earlier under its pergola. Served in chilled cups made of brightly painted ceramic, it was a treat for the eyes as well as being delicious. To go with it were small football-shaped black olives, a loaf of warm bread on a wooden cutting board and individual saucers of olive oil sprinkled with herbs for dipping the bread.

Dana was hungry. Though it might show a lack of sensitivity on her part, she couldn't pretend otherwise. The last time she'd eaten was hours ago on the plane, and then only a continental breakfast of an ice cold roll, lukewarm coffee and a green banana.

"So what do you think?" Andrea asked, leaning back in his chair across from her, his glass held in long, well-formed fingers. His gaze that rested on her face was intent, watchful.

"Very nice."

She meant that, actually. The bread was crisp on the outside, soft and moist on the inside, with a delectable yeasty aroma and taste. The combination of herbs in the olive oil was intriguing, and the olives themselves were plump and flavorful. The limoncello was a perfect accompaniment, cool, tart and sweetly refreshing.

"I'm glad you approve." The words were dry.

"Excuse me if I'm not as fervent as you might like, but it's the best I can do under the circumstances."

"Ah, yes, the circumstances. Are you licensed to operate a helicopter?"

She had thought he meant to ignore her gesture toward escape. She should have known better. She removed an olive pit from her mouth before she spoke.

"Not exactly."

"Not at all, or so I suspect."

She had taken the controls of one a couple of times while hanging out with a guy who piloted one of the police surveillance choppers. Not that she intended to share that information with Andrea.

"It didn't appear that difficult while you were doing it," she said, reaching for her glass again.

"So you would really have tried to take off."

"Did you leave it unlocked because you thought I wouldn't?"

"An oversight only, though I'm beginning to think there

is little you would not try." He went on with barely a pause. "To save future trouble for us both, I will tell you there is little chance of leaving the island without aid, but such assistance will not be forthcoming. Every person on the island is connected to my family in one way or another. I am in some ways the *padrone*, the master of the island as in days gone by. By now, all know I have a guest and will treat you with the utmost respect. However, no man will provide transport without my consent. They may smile and agree, but will come directly to me for authorization."

She gave him her deadliest stare. "How lovely for you."

"Convenient, anyway," he answered, unperturbed. "What is the point of having wealth if things cannot be arranged as you wish?"

"Having power, you mean."

"If you prefer."

"It sounds as if a reluctant guest is not unusual."

His chuckle was easy and rich with humor. "Believe it or not, you are the first."

"Lucky me."

She sipped her liqueur and then sat watching the swirl of alcohol in the yellow liquid. It was a surprisingly potent drink, so probably a way of persuading her to relax as he had suggested earlier. She could feel it seeping along her veins, encouraging that gentle effect, making her aware of how quiet it was here, and how peaceful the island seemed, at least on the surface.

She looked up, and was distracted for an instant by a shaft of sunlight falling through the grapevines overhead, touching the waves of Andrea's hair with molten light and gilding one chiseled plane of his face while leaving the other in shadow. The effect was so mesmerizing that her breath caught in her throat for a second. It was an effort to ignore the image enough to meet the concentration in his green eyes.

"I believe you were going to tell me how I earned this honor?"

"I was, wasn't I?" he answered, and then glanced beyond her. "But it will wait for later. Now we must eat."

Their food had arrived, it seemed, plates of pasta rich with a medley of seafood seasoned with garlic and parsley and glistening with olive oil.

Exasperation sang in Dana's veins as she leaned back in her chair to allow young Tommaso to serve her, to add ground pepper and parmesan to her plate and then pour dry white wine and cool mineral water. She had a feeling Andre was delaying his explanation, though why she could not imagine. She would let him get away with it for now, but not much longer.

Guaio appeared soon after the pasta, no doubt following the seafood scent from the kitchen or wherever he had been released from his carrier. He twined around her feet with imperious meows, obviously hopeful of sharing the meal. When she felt the rumble of what promised to be a demand, she chose a shrimp from her dish and gave it to him, though it was a wrench to part with it. The simple offering of pasta was one of the most delicious things she had ever tasted, though she kept the impression to herself.

Andrea pushed his plate aside after a few minutes, though a portion of his pasta remained. Taking up the bottle of wine Tommaso had left behind, he refilled their glasses. He drank from his then sat turning it in his hands. Finally, he set it back beside his plate. Squaring his shoulders, he rested his elbows on his chair arms and linked his fingers together.

"So. About why you are here with me."

Dana put down her fork with care and picked up her glass of mineral water. "Yes?"

"I told you Guaio belongs to my sister, yes?"

"You did."

"Isabella, or Bella as she in known in the family, is involved in a rather messy divorce. After some six years of marriage, she discovered her husband has, or did have, a mistress with a child. Rico swears the affair was over years ago, soon after they met, but Bella refuses to believe it. It is doubly hurtful for her because she and Rico have no children. Guaio was in some ways a substitute for the baby they both wanted but couldn't conceive. Both are now demanding custody."

"You mean they are fighting over a cat?"

His face remained serious. "It's something more than that. Bella believes Rico will do away with Guaio if he gets his hands on him."

"Surely not!"

"Who can say? I would have doubted it a month ago, but now Rico blames the cat for their breakup. He swears Bella never loved him as she does Guaio."

Dana set down her water glass without drinking from it. "Is he right?"

"It may be true Bella lavished as much money and attention on her pet as she might a child, but intense grooming is necessary for competition."

Guaio, finished with his shrimp, sat down and washed his face, pausing now and then to give Dana a hopeful stare. It almost seemed he knew he was the subject of their discussion.

Andrea glanced at the cat then forked a morsel of seafood from his plate and leaned to offer it. Guaio turned his head in feline disdain. Rising, he moved to rub his chin along Dana's shoe.

The urge toward one-upmanship was impossible to resist. Searching out another shrimp from her pasta was no great sacrifice as her appetite seemed to have fled. The cat took her offering with gratifying promptness.

She watched him a moment before sending a triumphant smile toward the man across from her.

"Anyway," he said, a stringent note in his voice, "Rico claims Bella took the cat to shows to avoid being with him, also to gain the prize money she needed for support after the divorce. The last is ridiculous, of course, as she has her inheritance from our father. And she can always apply to me for whatever she might need."

"Maybe she should just talk to her husband—"

"When they meet, they do nothing but quarrel." He lifted a shoulder. "I love my sister but she enjoys shouting and throwing things, and seldom sees any side of a question except her own. Rico is much the same, the kind of man who believes the person who shouts louder wins."

"Have they not noticed it isn't working?"

"Apparently that no longer matters. They have descended from shouting to threats. Now it appears they may have come to worse."

Dana was quiet a moment. "By that, you mean the attempt to run me down this morning."

"You were holding Guaio at the time, if you will remember. The idea was possibly to make you drop him."

"Drop him so he might be run over." She shivered a little at the chill brought on by that idea.

"If you wish to be charitable."

His level tone told her he thought the driver of the car could easily have flattened her along with the cat. Thinking back, she wasn't sure it was impossible. "So one of the two men was this Rico, your sister's husband?"

"More likely, both were hired by him. It would be foolish to be caught in such an act while the divorce is pending. The same men may have broken into Bella's house. At least someone came in through a window last night, but crossed an electric eye. They set off an alarm, so had to abandon their purpose."

"You are positive they were after the cat?"

"Bella is, and that is what matters. She called me to come immediately, to take Guaio and keep him with me, keep him safe until this is over."

"That's what you were doing this morning." If the cat belonged to his sister then it made sense Andrea was not that familiar with the animal, also that Guaio preferred a female as a caretaker.

Andrea inclined his head. "I was followed by those two in the sedan, as you know, but managed to stay ahead of them until the traffic jam."

She'd just bet he had, given the power of his Lamborghini. "What kind of man is this Rico that he'd go to such lengths? Is he crazy or just some kind of Neapolitan crook?"

"A member of the Cosa Nostra, you mean to say? By no means. He's only a husband who doesn't want to lose his wife, but has no clue how to keep her."

The look she sent him was cool. "Don't tell me you feel sorry for him."

He lifted a shoulder without answering. Picking up his wine glass again, he tossed back what was left in it.

"That's all well and good," Dana went on after a moment, "but I don't see what it has to do with me. I'm just a tourist with no ties to any of this."

"You are tied to me, at least in the minds of the two thugs who saw you today."

"That's ridiculous," she snapped, in spite of the odd ripple along her nerves at the idea. "They don't know who I am or where to find me."

"You were driving a car with a rental license plate, yes?"

"Well, but—"

"You used a credit card when you picked it up, or so I imagine. You were required to state your destination on the rental agreement. You provided a photo ID, such as your passport or driver's permit?"

She nodded with reluctance. She was well aware of the plastic trail people could leave behind them, but hadn't connected it to her own activities until this moment.

Guaio chose that moment to leap up into her lap. She caught him, steadied him with a thumb under his collar with its glittering blue stones, taking solace from the way he immediately settled in her lap and rumbled into a purr.

"Rico has a cousin who works with Interpol in an executive capacity. Italy is a country that thrives on the exchange of favors. Must I say more?"

"Even so, I'm not really involved," she said, keeping her gaze on the cat as she smoothed her hand down his back.

"I repeat, you were seen with me. They know you left the accident scene in my car. I can't guarantee you won't be targeted if only because these men may believe I would hand over Guaio in exchange for you."

She swallowed hard before looking up to meet his serious green gaze. "You mean they might try to turn me into some kind of hostage."

"It was once a favorite pastime in certain parts of Italy."

"That's insane!"

"This is not a sane time between Bella and Rico. They aren't themselves, I fear, aren't really responsible for the things they are saying and doing."

"Oh, please. People are always responsible."

A smile came and went across his face so quickly she wasn't sure she saw it. "Some people only, not all. But the fact is I would instantly give up Guaio in exchange for you, and that would break Bella's heart."

The oddest warmth poured along Dana's veins at the idea that he might value her comfort and safety above the life of his sister's pet cat. That was perfectly senseless when he only meant he would place a higher value on any human life. Still it held her silent as he went on.

"Hear me, then. You would not be in this predicament if I had remembered Guaio was with me when I stepped out of my car there at the traffic jam. You were quick enough, and kind enough, to rescue Bella's pet when he escaped, for which I am supremely grateful. But now it is my responsibility to make certain you don't regret that impulse. I will feel much better if you remain here where I can see to it you are kept safe."

"Oh, please."

"Yes, even if you think it is insanity," he went on in answer to her thought rather than what she'd said. "It is my hope you will agree it is a sensible precaution, and perhaps look on these next few days as a vacation, a holiday. It will be different from the one you had planned, yes, but a holiday all the same."

FOUR

*H*ad he convinced her?

Andrea could not tell. The flash of resentment in her eyes when he said she might consider her stay on the island as a holiday suggested it was unlikely.

She was a woman with a mind of her own. Another time he might relish matching wills and wits with her, but not now. She had cause to resent what he had done, but the situation would be more tolerable for them both if she could be persuaded to cooperate.

Making life tolerable for him would not be high on her list of priorities, he thought. In fact, she would probably take pleasure in making it as difficult as possible.

She was doing that already, if she only knew. All she had to do was turn her head so the sunlight struck fire from hair or slanted across the freckle-dusted planes of her face, and the pants he wore became as uncomfortable as she could wish.

Would she really have tried to take off in the helicopter if he had not put a stop to it? He feared she might have. It didn't bear thinking about, as she could easily have spun into a free fall that landed her in the sea. He could feel sweat break out across the back of his neck at the mere thought.

He must watch her like a hawk with a snake in its nest. It would be no hardship, this close surveillance, but he could already see its hidden dangers.

She sat across from him now, slowly smoothing her hand along the thick fur on Guaio's back while the cat closed his eyes to slits and kneaded her jean-clad knee in ecstasy. It was just a little annoying when Bella's pet would have nothing to do with him. He'd taken care of the animal as if it were a child, but earned only disdain. All Dana had done was feed him a shrimp or two and he appeared to have bonded with her for life.

Look at that, the two of them were even yawning in unison. It was almost comical.

"Sleepy?" Andrea asked.

"A little. I never sleep well on planes."

"You landed at Naples this morning after an overseas flight, yes? You must be exhausted. There's no reason you shouldn't lie down if you like. Half the island does the same after lunch."

Her smile was a little crooked. "Only half? I thought the whole of Italy shut down between one and four in the afternoon."

"Very near it," he conceded.

"But not you."

"I abandoned the habit some years ago. Much of my business occurs in places where such an afternoon break isn't practical."

"And I never formed it in the first place. Besides, if I sleep now I'll be wide awake in the middle of the night. It will be better if I adjust to Italian time."

Her refusal was hardly surprising since resting had been his suggestion. He should have told her it would better if she didn't nap. Then she might have allowed herself that small concession.

It was his private opinion that she should adjust to more that was Italian than the time zone and afternoon rest. She was entirely too tense, too prickly in her independence. He wondered what it would take, other than limoncello, to induce her to let go and let things happen as they would.

What might it take to have her become his willing guest?

"Would you care to see more of the island then?" he asked as courteously as he was able. "I have a few things to look after while I am here. I could give you the grand tour at the same time."

She met his gaze as if seeking an ulterior motive to the invitation. He held that long look, his own as clear as his conscience.

"That sounds nice," she said finally.

Nice.

Andrea was not sure what he expected, but would have been glad of a little more enthusiasm. "Excellent. I'll have a golf cart brought around."

"Golf cart?"

"My great-grandfather banned gas-powered vehicles on the island. They were too fast and too noisy, so he said, and the island so small a man could walk from one end to the other in a few hours. He kept a donkey cart for his use, but I am not so dedicated to tradition."

She almost smiled at that droll observation. It was such a pleasant look, such a rewarding result, that he set himself the challenge of making her do it again.

The golf cart was top-of-the-line, but still none-too-large. Andrea was well aware of that drawback; in fact he depended upon it. Watching Dana take the far side of the narrow seat and wedge herself in place with her feet against the floorboard, he hid a smile. The cart track that criss-crossed the island was steep and winding, having been constructed following what was once a goat track. She would be close against him before she knew it.

"Hold up!"

That cry came from Dana before the cart moved off a dozen feet. Glancing back, he saw Guaio trotting after them with his tail waving over his back.

Dana had put him down before she left the terrace. It was amazing to see the pampered feline expend the energy to follow after her, Andrea thought, even as he braked for the cat.

Guaio needed no coaxing to join them. He leaped at once to Dana's lap.

"You will be too hot," Andrea said in warning.

"Will I?" She held the cat up so she could look into the

slits that centered his blue eyes. "What do you think, sir?"

The answer to her question was a rather meek meow.

"Perhaps you are right, my feline friend. Onto the back seat with you then."

It was a miniscule victory, this acceptance of his advice, but Andrea would take whatever encouragement he could get. He waited until the cat was settled. Then he took off again.

They zipped over the hillsides with the wind in their hair and warm sun slanting in under the cart's fiberglass top to slide over their faces. Andrea lifted a hand to acknowledge the waves of islanders is their garden patches, women pegging laundry on clothes lines where it flapped in the constant sea breeze, and children playing in dooryards. A trio of boys chased after them on their bikes, caught up with them long enough to yell a greeting and receive one in return, and fell back, out of breath.

They passed above the town, looking down on its tumble of buildings in colors softened to rainbow pastels by sun and salt water. It was a scene so familiar Andrea seldom noticed it, though it seemed picturesque today as he looked at it from Dana's perspective. The roof of the community center needed repairing, just as his housekeeper had informed him, and the football field could use new fencing. He must see to these things. The owner of the new restaurant should be warned to dispose of his trash, as well.

All these things fell to his lot, not that he minded. It was the tradition so could not be avoided.

The town curved to follow the shape of the harbor, with

a marina at its center. Colored an intense blue with only a hint of green, the anchorage was deep enough to support the usual fishing boats and give shelter to an occasional yacht during storms. A few sailboats bobbed and swayed beyond the breakwater, but there was nothing in that for concern, certainly nothing to cause alarm.

This was the main landing for the island. The remaining coastline was too steep and rocky to be safe. That didn't make access impossible.

It was a moment before he realized his passenger had leaned forward, holding to the low windshield as she gazed past him.

"You are okay, the swaying of the cart doesn't bother you?" he asked.

"Not at all. Should it?"

"It affects some."

She gave him a steady stare. "Is there something you're looking for down there?"

"Something. Anything. Everything." He spoke almost at random while squinting against the sun glare on the water. A boat he didn't recognize lay offshore, drifting with the current. From this distance, he couldn't tell if the two figures in it were there to swim, enjoy the sun and the water, or something more. The craft was fair-sized and built for speed rather than fishing, which seemed a bit suspicious.

Sliding his cell phone from his pocket, he thumbed the screen, touched a number and gave a quiet order. With this taken care of, he moved on again.

"What was that about?"

"A precaution only." He deliberately did not look back at the drifting boat before he continued almost at random. "Tell me how you became a policewoman. Was there nothing else you could have done?"

"What's wrong with the police?"

He sent her an appraising glance. "You don't seem the type."

"And what type might that be?"

He wasn't about to get into that. "Was your father perhaps in law enforcement?"

"And my two brothers," she said shortly.

At least he had teased a little information from her. 'You come from a large family then?"

"Not really, only two boys and one girl, with the last being me, of course."

"But you are close?"

"Close enough they will wonder what's wrong if they don't hear from me soon. My mother, in particular, is a worrier."

"You must call her then," he said promptly. He didn't know if what she'd said was true or a subtle warning, but it didn't matter. His point was she was not being denied contact with the world beyond the island.

"If I say the word, she will see to it my brothers are on the first plane for Italy."

He tilted his head. "Am I supposed to be intimidated?"

"At the very least," she said stoutly.

"Sorry. But you would tell your mama to send them where?"

She met his gaze, the light in her dark brown eyes as assessing as his own must have been moments before. "I expect they could figure out that part, once they have your name. If the island has been in the family as long as you say, its ownership can hardly be a secret."

That was correct, unfortunately. "But then they would have no jurisdiction here, no authority of any kind."

"Except what they may take for themselves."

"Like that, are they? If so, I might welcome them as rein-forcements."

"Might you now?"

She didn't believe him. Ah, well, Andrea wasn't sure he believed it himself. He had no wish for their privacy to be interrupted, not just yet. No, and maybe not at all.

"Your English seems to be improving," she said abruptly. "How is that?"

"Extra use, I suppose," he answered with a quick glance in her direction. "Give me another day or two, and I may develop a Southern drawl."

She gave a short laugh. "That would be awful."

"I don't know. Yours is intriguing, even—sexy."

Color came and went under the pale red-head skin of her face with its dusting of freckles, though she seemed unaware of it. "But yours is fine just the way it is."

He drew back as if insulted. "Mine? I have no accent!"

"No, and birds don't fly." Her soft chuckle died away. "Just how many languages do you speak?"

"Only five, with a smattering of Greek."

She pretended to groan. "*Only* five or six."

"Well, and a little Japanese. Enough to find my way around Tokyo without starving."

"Stop it. Bragging is unbecoming."

He laughed at her look of disgust, even as he swerved onto a track that would take them to the far end of the island. The movement pressed her thigh against his from hip to knee, a warm firmness that made him think of the tender inner skin of those thighs, and how they would feel clamped upon him.

"Languages are a knack," he answered in distraction, "like counting cards or memorizing knitting patterns."

She rolled her eyes. "What do you know about knitting?"

"Bella is a knitter. She is never without something on her needles as she claims it soothes her nerves."

"Are the two of you all there are?"

Her question was only a polite attempt to keep the conversation going, Andrea thought, but answered anyway. "In the immediate family, yes. Our parents divorced when we were teenagers. Our mother went back to her family in Rome and our father retreated here. He died a year or two later in a boating accident. It was the two of us, Andrea and Bella, against the world."

"And still is, or so it appears to me."

She was right, not that he intended to admit it. As they topped a rise and saw the sea spread out as far as the eye could reach, he swung the cart in a half circle and came to a halt.

"What is this?" she asked, glancing around. "Why are we stopping?"

"This is the end of the line."

"You mean—Oh, I see, it's the far end of the island."

He gave a slow, disbelieving shake of his head. "What did you think I meant?"

She hunched a shoulder without answering.

She could not really have thought he meant to toss her over the edge of the headland? Could she? Andrea frowned at the thought. He must try harder to reassure her.

Scooting away from him, perhaps from the heat of his body against hers, she stepped from the golf cart and walked to the cliff's edge. The wind caught the oversized shirt she wore, making it balloon around her. She crossed her arms over her chest and grabbed the excess knit fabric, holding it tight around her body.

Andrea's gaze was welded to the sight as he eased from the cart and followed after her. She didn't intend anything by it, yet the tightly pulled shirt defined the svelte line of her back as it flowed into the curves of her hips in a way that set the blood to boiling in his veins. He wanted to trace the gentle shape with his hands, follow it with lips and tongue, cover it with his body. It was astounding, the power of that need.

It was so mind-boggling, in fact, that he failed to notice the boat that skimmed toward them until it was less than a hundred yards away. It was sleek and white and left only a narrow white line for a wake. Two men stood in the cockpit.

One of them was steering, though his gaze was fastened on Andrea and Dana where they stood on top of the cliff-like headland. The other had a rifle in hands.

The deadly shape of the weapon was unmistakable. So was the movement as he lifted it to his shoulder.

~ ~ ~

"Down!"

The hard-voiced shout came from Andrea. Dana was already on the ground, rolling once, twice as a shot rang out behind her. She came up in scuttle position, making a bee-line toward the golf cart.

Andrea was right behind her, shielding her as they ran. They veered apart as they reached the small vehicle, him taking the driver's side, her sprinting for the other. She slid inside with such force her shoulder slammed into his ribs as he did the same. She winced but wrenched away from him so he could set the cart in motion.

He wheeled it in a wide arc and sent it careening away back down the track. Dana twisted this way and that, looking for Guaio. The cat was on the floorboard at her feet, crouched half under the seat with his ears laid back. Only when she was sure he was safe did she turn in her seat to look toward the sea behind them.

A fishing trawler was bearing down upon the speed boat. Easily ten times its size, it pushed a huge bow wave ahead of it as it roared through the water. With its high prow and greater weight, it could easily cut the smaller boat in half.

The cavalry had arrived, or so it seemed.

The men in the speed boat had seen it, for they had sheared off with an arching plume of water, racing away like a rabbit with a hound after it. The gunman must have dropped down behind the windscreen for he was no longer in sight.

"They're leaving," she said over her shoulder. "A fishing boat chased them off."

Andrea spared a quick backward glance while muttering something under his breath.

A moment later, the rise of the headland cut off Dana's view of the sea. She settled into her seat again, swinging to face him.

"What did you say?"

"Nothing. Just that it's about time someone showed up."

She studied the tense set of his features and the stiffness of his shoulders while aromatic shrubs, an ancient olive grove and the ruins of a stone cottage whipped past barely noticed. "That's who you called," she said finally. "You ordered that fishing boat to patrol the island."

"A precaution only," he answered with a short nod. "I didn't expect to be shot at."

"Just what did you expect?"

He shrugged without answering.

That was a male habit Dana despised when her brothers tried it. "Someone coming in close enough to watch the villa maybe?" she asked in exasperation. "Guys in black rappelling up a cliff face to kidnap Guaio out of his carrier? What?"

"I'm not sure. I just didn't like the look of them."

"Neither did I, but—"

He turned his head to look at her, slowing the cart at the same time. "But what?"

"I don't see what they expected to gain. I mean, I'm not familiar with the island or even this part of the world, but landing a boat below where we were standing looked to be a dicey proposition. As for firing the rifle, the chance of actually hitting one of us was next to zero from a moving boat and with that high angle."

"Next to zero is still too close," he said drily.

"I suppose the point could have been to deliver a message. If so, they must not know you well."

He gave a short laugh. "No? Because?"

"You're far too arrogant to be easily intimidated." She went on without waiting for a reply. "Regardless, this business seems to involve a ridiculous amount of muscle and firepower for a cat."

"Even one as superior as Guaio?"

She could become addicted to the glint of humor that lurked half-hidden in his eyes most of the time. Yes, in spite of her irritation. "Or a dozen more like him."

"Heaven forbid there should be such a thing. I do agree it's time I talk to Bella, find out her ideas about what's going on. As irrational as Rico can be at times, it's hard to believe he would go this far."

"Well, but if it's not Rico behind it, who else could it be?"

"That is the question," he answered, all trace of humor gone from his voice.

The quiet that settled between them was broken only by the electric hum of the cart, the whisper of its tires on the paved track and the distant cries of gulls that circled above the island. The sun was warm on Dana's face and the breeze like gentle fingers as it ruffled through her hair.

Slowly, the adrenaline faded from her bloodstream to be replaced by a strange lassitude. The harrowing moments back there on the headland seemed surreal, like a bad dream that vanished on awakening.

She grew steadily more aware of the man beside her, of his scent of clean linen, subtle men's cologne and fresh air. Her shoulder where it brushed his arm as they were jostled by the uneven pathway seemed super-sensitive, so she felt every movement of his muscles. Her thigh tingled along its length where it touched his, a sensation that radiated through her with disturbing power.

What was the matter with her? She wasn't some silly teenager who could be swayed by an autocratic manner and awesomely masculine face. She was no thrill-seeker turned on by the possibility that she might have been brought to the island for something more than the promise of a safe haven.

If somewhere deep inside that seemed a shame, she wasn't about to let such a reckless idea influence her.

Well, all right, she'd been given an explanation that seemed plausible, even if a little off-the-wall. She could talk to her family whenever she elected. Though fairly confident of her ability to protect herself, she was neither stupid nor egotistical enough to suppose she could fight off men with guns while she was unarmed.

The semi-confinement would only be for a day or two at most, until the situation could be changed. Would it really be such a bad thing to accept a few days of down time on a private island?

Yes. Yes, it would.

She should have been given a choice. What would have been so hard about explaining the situation in the beginning and letting her decide if she wanted the protection only a high-powered billionaire could provide?

Of course, she wouldn't have taken it. There was no way Andrea Tonello could have convinced her it was necessary just a few hours ago.

Dana glanced at him as he sent the cart flying back toward the villa, noting his patrician nose, chiseled mouth, and eyes so narrowed in concentration that his lashes meshed at the corners. High-handed, macho, superior Italian. She wasn't ready to forgive him, no matter how many times she was threatened or shot at. He didn't deserve it, for one thing, but that wasn't all. She couldn't let down her guard, not now, maybe not ever. She didn't dare as it seemed likely getting too close to Andrea might well be more dangerous than anything else.

A curve appeared ahead of them, a sharp bend around what appeared to be roadside shrine of some kind. Andrea took it as if driving in the Le Mans, cutting it so short the cart tilted on two wheels. Dana, thrown off balance, slid on the seat, ramming her shoulder against his elbow. A short cry left her, and she grabbed at the spot with her free hand.

"What is it?" he demanded, his gaze probing. "You weren't hit by one of the rounds back there?"

"No, I don't—" She stopped in sudden recognition. "It's just the place where Guaio held on while we dodged the car this morning."

"He clawed you?"

"I guess you could call it that, though he didn't mean to do it."

Exasperation crossed Andrea's face as he sent a quick look toward where Guaio crouched at their feet. "Why didn't you say so? Cat scratches are known for getting infected. That should have been cleaned and taken care of at once."

"I know that," she returned with some ire. "My first aid kit was in my suitcase. Besides, I've been busy being abducted."

"Not that busy." The incredulous look she gave him seemed not to faze him at all, for he went on at once. "Never mind, I'll look at this injury when we reach the villa."

"I'll take care of it," she said with precision, "if you can provide antibiotic cream and a Band-Aid."

He didn't answer. She hoped that meant he agreed with her intention, but somehow doubted it.

The villa was in an uproar when they arrived back at the front entrance. Apparently Andrea's instructions for the fishing boat had been instantly transmitted to every soul on the island, as had the news that rifle shots had been fired. He was met with cries of outraged sympathy, voluble questions and much waving of hands.

Dana skirted the hubbub, making for the room she had been allotted. She was about to close the door behind her when she realized she'd been followed. Guaio, meowing loudly, padded after her and slid around the door. Once there, he leaped to the mattress of her bed, turned around twice, and lay down in the middle. From there he regarded her with interest, as if to ask just where she intended to lie down.

"You, sir, are a—a *guaio*," she told him with mock severity. "What makes you think I want your company, tell me that?"

The cat blinked, and then yawned.

"Yes, I know you missed your nap, but whose fault is that? I didn't tell you to join us for the island tour. If you got more than you bargained for, don't come complaining to me."

Guaio rolled to his back, twitching his rear end from side to side to hollow out his place of rest. Satisfied with its depth, he flopped to his side and closed his eyes.

"Just like a guy," Dana said with a laugh. "Fine. Go to sleep while I'm still talking to you."

The cat didn't even open an eyelid. Turning away with a shake of her head, she moved into the bathroom. She thought she heard a noise a few minutes later, but decided it was probably Guaio jumping from the bed. She had picked up her brush to remove the tangles from her wind-blown hair when it came again.

"What is it with you?" she scolded as she emerged from the bathroom. "Can't I have a minute to ... to myself?"

Her voice died away as she saw Andrea standing in the door with one hand on the knob and the other holding a small tray set with of what appeared to be medical supplies. Heat burned across her cheekbones, creeping into her hairline.

"Apparently not. Or at least not yet," he said, his voice even as he answered her complaint.

"I was talking to the cat." She raked the brush through her hair since it gave her something to do other than stand there feeling ridiculous.

"Were you? I could be wrong, but I don't believe he is going to answer."

That was true enough. Guaio had rolled to his back again and was sound asleep with his feet sticking up in the air. "We were having a nice conversation before, but I suppose he had an exhausting day."

"He isn't the only one. If you'll let me look at these scratches of yours first, we'll see about unwinding a bit."

She stepped forward with her hand outstretched. "Thanks, but I can take care of it."

"I would prefer to make certain there is no infection as I feel responsible. If you'll remove your shirt—"

"That won't be necessary. I've been tending my own cuts and scrapes for quite a while now." She threw the hairbrush onto the bed and shook back her hair.

"Bullet wounds and other minor injuries, I suppose. You just patch them up and keep working."

"I didn't say that."

"But these cuts and scrapes were in the line of duty?"

She closed her eyes and then opened them again. "There's no need for you to be concerned, okay? I know a simple scratch when I see it."

"So do I, which is why I'd like to take a look. We can stand here and argue all day, but I am not going away. It will be much simpler if you will just let me help you."

She couldn't force him to leave, and something inside her prevented the screaming fit that might make him retreat. It went against the grain to give in, yet the marks on her shoulder burned and throbbed as if there might be something going on with them.

What did it matter, anyway? It wasn't as if she thought he had designs on her body, or would be inflamed by the sight of her bare shoulder or even her favorite peach-colored lace bra.

The sooner this was over, the better. She could finally have a little privacy.

"Oh, all right," she snapped. Crossing her arms at her waist, she grabbed the bottom edge of his rust-colored T-shirt she wore and whipped it off over her head.

His eyes widened a fraction, but he said not a word. His gaze moved slowly over her torso from her neck to her waist, scarcely pausing on the pale and soft yet resilient curves rising from their lace covering. It rested on her flat, taut abdomen before trailing down to where her jeans hugged her thighs.

"Well?"

She put as much bravado as she could scrape together into that single word, but it did nothing to prevent the flush that mottled her damnably fair skin. Shaking out the polo shirt, she spread it over her chest for cover, tucking the edges under her arms.

"Well, indeed."

He swallowed, a clear movement in the strong column of

his neck, before meeting her sardonic gaze. "If you will sit over there?"

At least he hadn't asked her to lie on the bed. That was one pitfall avoided.

Dana sank into the chair and turned to the side so her injured shoulder could be reached. Tilting her head, she gathered her hair in one hand and held it out of the way.

Andrea came forward, going to one knee beside the chair. He inspected her shoulder, touched it gently.

His fingers were cool in contrast to the warmth of her skin. A shiver ran over Dana, prickling her arms and back with goose bumps. She willed them to subside while catching the inside of her bottom lip between her teeth.

Such a light, impersonal touch had never affected her that way before. The scratches must be feverish already. That was it.

He set the medical tray on a side table and selected a bottle and gauze pads. Seconds later, the pungent smell of some iodine-based wash rose around them.

Dana's breath hissed between her teeth as he swiped over the scratches.

"Sorry," he murmured without pausing in what he was doing. "It will only hurt for a second."

Her traitorous mind went skipping to another scenario where he might have said such a thing. What would it have been like to have him whisper those words against her ear in his velvety voice with its delectable trace of an accent? She could feel the nipples of her breasts contracting, and prayed it wasn't noticeable under both bra and draped shirt.

Or if it was, that he would attribute it to surprise, pain, chill—anything except its true cause.

"It's okay," she said after a moment. "Just get on with it."

He did that all right, scrubbing over the scratches with thorough care. To aid that effort, he closed his other hand around her upper arm, holding her steady. His grasp was warm and sure, not at all tight, and yet inescapable. The sad thing was she wasn't sure she wanted to escape.

It was excruciating, trying to ignore what he was doing, waiting to see what he would do next. She needed something, anything, to counteract the wildly inappropriate feelings inside her.

"When are the police arriving?" she asked in strained tones.

He flicked a glance at her set face before returning his attention to his job. "They aren't."

"Even after someone shot at us? That makes no sense!"

"We weren't hit and the boat is long gone. There's no proof shots was fired, no way to identify the shooter. I could ask for the *guardia costiera* to patrol the waters around the island or hire guards for the villa, but to what end? My own people can do the job just as well, maybe better."

"What, there are no laws against vigilante tactics in Italy?" Her police training, policeman's attitude, sparked that question.

"The concept originated in America, I believe. Even there, a man is permitted some leeway in protecting his home and property. And I would remind you that I own the island."

He was so calmly logical. It was one of the most irritating things about him. "You don't think it might be useful to file a report in case you or someone else is forced to shoot an intruder?"

"Maybe." He met her gaze an instant before looking back to her shoulder. "But any official account would likely be in the hands of some tabloid by dark. My sister would not be happy to have the details of her divorce discussed over the breakfast tables of Europe."

"Oh, well, better to be dead than the subject of gossip," she said in brittle disparagement.

"Some perceive it so." He set aside the gauze squares he'd been using and opened a package that seemed to hold a large adhesive bandage. He squeezed a generous amount of some ointment on it, and then placed it carefully on her shoulder.

"Considering how many people on the island know about what took place, it can't be long before the world hears about it."

"They will not betray family matters. More than that, they know there is a problem, not its cause."

"No? Then who do they think the gunman was after?"

He only looked at her, his expression grave.

"Well—" she began then stopped. "No. No way."

He returned his hooded gaze to what he was doing. "You were there. It makes sense."

"Not to me, it doesn't!"

"All right, it makes sense for now, until I can get to the

bottom of this affair between Bella and Rico."

"That's all very well, but in the meantime, your sister isn't the one in danger."

"She isn't," he said as he pressed the edges of the bandage down with the firm, even pressure of his fingertips. "Not yet."

She tipped her head to peer into his face, disturbed by something in his voice. "But you believe she might be?"

"It seems possible? That's if it was Rico who sent the thugs we've dealt with so far."

"All the more reason to go to the police."

He shifted a shoulder. "Unlike you, my faith in the ability of the police to keep any of us safe is limited."

"You think you can do better. But what if you are wrong?"

He didn't answer. Gathering up the trash he'd caused but leaving the tray of supplies, he got to his feet. "Does that feel better now?"

"Actually it does. Thank you."

"Glad to be of service." His smile was rueful before he spoke again. "I thought, perhaps, to have a swim. You might join me, but it would be better if the bandage remains dry. You could sit on the terrace, enjoy a drink and watch the sun go down."

"You don't have to entertain me."

"But I do," he corrected instantly. "I am your host, therefore it's my duty."

"Oh, your duty. And here I was thinking you just wanted to keep an eye on me."

A smile curled one corner of his mouth. "That too. Will you come?"

She was tired of sparring with him, tired of strife and the constant need to assert her independence. She was tired, period. Yet if she remained here, she would soon be as sound asleep as Guaio. And that would not do.

"Fine," she said. "I'll be there in a second."

He watched her for a long assessing moment. Then he reached to catch hold of the shirt she held against her, tugging it from her grasp. Turning it right side out, he gathered it in his hands and slipped the neck over her head, holding it as she found the sleeves and pushed her arms into them.

The backs of his fingers brushed the curves of her breasts as he lowered the hem. She stilled, and then leaned away from him, pulling the shirt into place as quickly as possible. When that was done, she met his gaze, her own steady as she waited to see what he might do next.

The heat of his gaze darkened his eyes to a green so deep it was almost black. "I could," he said quietly, "kiss it and make it well."

The idea was far too enticing for comfort, particularly as she had no idea where he meant to place this kiss. She lifted her chin. "I'm sure it will be fine without that."

"Too bad." His gaze rested on her face a moment longer before he turned away. He moved to the door, then, holding it open for her.

He meant to wait for her, leaving her no time to pull what was left of her composure around her. Dana turned and dragged Guaio from his comfortable place on her bed.

He meowed in protest, hanging boneless in her arms.

She paid no attention. Holding the cat in front of her like a shield, she marched from the room.

FIVE

*A*ndrea saw to it Dana was supplied with a chilled limoncello as she lay back on the chaise lounge with a stack of glossy magazines beside her. Something to soothe her nerves after what had happened must be beneficial.

She might not seem particularly stressed, but that was because she held everything inside her, he thought. Small things gave her away, a catch in her voice, a hint of fire in her eyes, the ripple of goose bumps she could not control. Whatever had happened to her, whatever she might feel, was his fault entirely. The least he could do was try to remedy it.

And if he needed more than one mildly alcoholic limoncello to soothe his irritation, this was not a problem. Tommaso would bring them until told to stop.

It wasn't just the threat from the men in the boat that annoyed him. He was also appalled by his own actions.

What had possessed him to go to her room? It was something more than a need to see the damage Guaio had caused, though that had been real enough. His urge to be close to her, to touch her had been just as strong.

Yes, she was naturally a little distant. Yes, it bothered him, and yes, he had an Italian's instinct to move deeper into her private space than might be comfortable for her as an American. Regardless, he should have known it could not be forced. Any man who got inside Dana's guard would have to coax her to open up to him. Rushing her would only cause her defenses to shut down tight.

And yet, how long did he have for that persuasion? He could not keep her here forever.

Per Dio, but she was so beautifully formed, with lovely curves added to the muscular firmness of her body, so tender beneath the toughness of her spirit. The contrast fascinated him.

He had been in her company barely a day and she was already driving him mad. He had not been so uncontrollably aroused by a woman since he was a teenager walking around half-crazed by testosterone and fantasies of female nakedness. It was as amazing as it was disturbing.

He drank one limoncello while changing into his usual black speedo in the pool house. Wearing a terrycloth robe over it that would serve as a towel, he carried a second ceramic cup of the tart, sweet drink with him as he returned to where he had left Dana.

She was still on the chaise lounge. Seeing her there, he breathed a little easier. Though he thought she was beginning to accept that it would be unwise as well as difficult to leave the island, he wouldn't put it past her to try.

The heat of the day was waning as the sun slipped down the sky, but it was still quite warm. Dana appeared far from comfortable in her jeans and his heavy shirt. That was before he noticed the cat lying at her side.

Guaio could not be removed without considerable trouble, and would no doubt return the first chance he got. The other problem he could solve with ease.

Andrea dropped down on the chaise next to hers and took out his cell phone from his robe pocket. "What are you favorite colors?" he asked with brisk efficiency. "Greens? Shades of blue? Peach-pink, perhaps?"

It was wrong of him to bring up the last, but he couldn't help it. The memory of her lace bra that was almost flesh-colored, also the tender curves it hugged, was too fresh. Besides, he was becoming addicted to watching her blush. He wondered if she realized the soft color not only appeared on her face and ears, but on her throat and even her breasts. He also wondered how far it descended, though unsure he would ever discover the answer.

"I like all colors," she said warily, "except maybe orange."

"*Bene*, this makes it simple." Finding the number he wanted in his contacts, he thumbed it in.

"What are you doing?"

"Calling the boutique in Positano that is my sister's favorite when she's here on holiday. You have nothing to wear except the clothes you have on. This will not do."

"I'd have plenty of clothes if I could get my suitcase back."

"A process that will take time. I must see to your well-being now."

"My well-being is fine. Besides, you might ask if I want anything else to wear before arranging my life for me."

He met the coolness in her eyes as he the listened to the phone ring on the other end. "*Signorina* Marsden," he said in the most polite tones he could manage, "would you care to have something more comfortable to wear, or would you rather live in what you have on—which I would guess you have been wearing for most of two days and a night now. This rather warm ensemble can be laundered, during which time I will gladly share my wardrobe. Or you may treat the island as your personal nude beach. I don't mind either way."

She gave him a dark look as color surged into her face once more. "Yes, all right, since you put it that way. But I can still buy my own."

"With what if I may ask? Unless you have a credit card tucked into your pocket?"

"No, but I can certainly pay you back. And I can make my own choices, thank you very much."

He held her determined gaze until a tinny voice in his ear snagged his attention.

"*Pronto*," he said into the phone. "*Un momento, per favore.*" Without another syllable, he handed it to Dana.

She took it gingerly, slipping it under her hair to hold it

to her ear before she spoke. Her face changed.

Andrea could hear the metallic rattle of Italian she could not understand. Strangely enough, the look of defeat that seeped into her face gave him no pleasure whatever.

Dana shoved the phone back at him. He took it with grave courtesy.

"*Mi dispiace*, I'm sorry, *cara*. Tell me what you want and the sizes you need, and I will translate."

She told him, and Andrea dutifully relayed the extremely short list. However, he multiplied the number for every item by six, and then added a bit more while keeping a wary eye on the dawning suspicion in Dana's face.

"What are you saying?" she demanded.

"Delivery instructions," he answered in a quick aside. He then added a nightgown and robe with matching slippers, a bikini in sea green and two pairs of thong sandals to the jeans, T-shirts and shorts she'd requested.

"I don't believe you."

"What else would it be?"

Such instructions had certainly been involved. With such a good excuse for continuing, he included a selection of cosmetics and hair products and a bottle of perfume.

She shot out a hand toward the phone as if she meant to take it from him. "That's enough, whatever you just said."

"I believe it may be." He smiled as he leaned away to avoid her grasp while expressing his thanks to the saleswoman. Ending the call, he threw off his short robe and slipped the cell phone back into the pocket before tossing it over the lounger. "I'm going into the pool now. Are you sure you will be all right here."

"Go, go." She waved him away while picking up a magazine, perhaps as an excuse not to look at him in his speedo. "Nothing is going to happen if you aren't on guard every minute."

His grandfather would have made the sign of the evil eye or else spat through his fingers at that blithe statement. Andrea would not go that far, though he was tempted. It was not wise to dare the devil.

He hit the water in a fast, shallow dive, coming up halfway across the long pool. For the next half hour, he swam as if the fiends of hell were after him, tearing up and down to wear off the adrenaline left over from the incident on the headland. That it also helped subdue his growing need to do more than merely guard his guest was surely all to the good.

Dana was asleep when he finally surged up onto the side of the pool and climbed out. She didn't stir as he picked up his robe from the chaise where he'd left it and dried his face. With it in his hands, he stood gazing down at her.

The lingering twilight that came as the sun went down had slowly turned to dusk darkness. Even in that dim light, her hair seemed to glow. There was such purity in her features that it sent an odd, half-forgotten tenderness curling around his heart. He had an almost irresistible urge to kneel beside her and wake her with a kiss.

He might have if Guaio hadn't been stretched out alongside her, watching him with unblinking distrust.

The cat had good reason, of course.

It would be as well, Andrea thought, to let Dana sleep.

She was jet-lagged and exhausted, and there would be plenty of time for her to adjust to Italian hours. He would return to wake her later, when he had showered and changed.

By the time he left his room again, the helicopter had arrived with the order from the boutique, settling onto the well-lit helipad built to accept a second chopper along with his that sat there.

The noise roused Dana, no doubt, for she was sitting up when he rejoined her on the terrace. The lights in the pool also had been turned on, as had those that marked the terrace levels and steps. The accusing look she turned on him was easily seen in their glow.

"Don't you look spiffy," she said in aggrieved tones as she allowed her gaze to rest briefly on the black pants he wore with a gray polo shirt and black sandals.

"*Grazie.*" It was ridiculous how pleased he was she'd noticed, no matter how it might be expressed.

"So how long did you leave me out here, dead to the world?"

"Not that long," he returned in soothing tones before nodding toward the helipad. "The order from the boutique has been delivered. If you like, you may now also look—ah, spiffy."

"You mean it's here? Already?"

She didn't sound at all excited as she turned toward where Luisa and Tommaso were carrying boxes into the house that had been offloaded from the arriving heli-copter. He might have known, though he hoped she would be pleased when she saw their contents. "I asked for immediate delivery in case you wanted to change before dinner, though this is not necessary in any way."

"It's dinnertime then?"

A corner of his mouth tilted in a sympathetic smile for the confusion in her eyes, as if she was a little disoriented from her nap as well as being unused to the level of service he commanded. "Not for an hour or so, perhaps more," he answered. "You must take all the time you wish to make ready."

"I'd rather not keep anyone waiting," she said, and pushed off the chaise.

Andrea put out a hand to catch her in case she was unsteady on her feet. She didn't require his aid, but gave him a small smile of appreciation anyway. A moment later, she walked away into the villa.

He stood quite still with his gaze on the straight line of her back, the slight sway of her hips, the way her hair moved on her shoulders. It was only after she disappeared through the doorway that he realized he was still holding out his hand as if trying to keep her with him.

~ ~ ~

It was too much, the clothing sent from the boutique, all of it ultra-chic and far more expensive than was at all necessary.

Dana stood with her hands on her hips, staring at the items strewn over her bed, unearthed from the tissue-paper lined boxes that were now stacked on the floor. The jeans sported designer labels and would fit like a second skin. The T-shirts were adorned with tucks and ruffles, buttons and bling. There were linen sheaths with matching jackets in pastel colors which she'd certainly never ordered, and more bits of lingerie than she'd owned in her life. Added to the clothing was a gorgeous cosmetic bag containing enough makeup and hair products for a half dozen females.

She wasn't going to be on the island long enough to wear a fraction of what lay before her.

Was she?

It would have to be sent back. That's all there was to it. She could barely afford even one of the T-shirts, much less all the rest.

Why couldn't Andrea have just done as she asked? She was sick of the jeans she had on, longed to be clean from the skin out. Once she'd come to terms with the idea of him ordering clothes for her, she'd begun to look forward to showering and changing.

He had thought to add a hairbrush to the list. Amazing. She touched a fingertip to the polished wooden handle, ran it over the boar bristles.

And perfume, too. Without any real intention of using it, she picked up the small spray bottle, removed its gold cap and sent a fine mist of the scent into the air.

Lovely, and exactly what she would have chosen if she'd been willing to splurge on real perfume in the first place. She'd never used anything other than cologne in her life.

Resolutely, she put the perfume bottle down. She picked up a T-shirt in pale lime green with a design in pink and blue brilliants around the scooped neckline, seeing that it matched a pair of crop pants in white with lime cuffs edged with more brilliants.

She put it down again.

No.

She couldn't.

Yet Andrea had looked so very handsome on the terrace just now, with his impeccable grooming and casual-chic shirt and pants. Not that he'd been as stunning as in that miniscule black speedo; the sight of him poised on the side of the pool, every long, perfect muscle gilded by sunlight, might be permanently imprinted in her mind. But still. She really hated the idea of sitting down to dinner in what she had on. Truth to tell, it was not only a little grubby but no longer fresh after being on her body so long.

Maybe if she chose a couple of the plainest outfits and just one of the lovely sheath dresses she wouldn't have to take out a major loan to pay for them?

When she appeared in the living room a half hour later, she wore a peach linen sheath and a pair of thong sandals with their vamps set with pearls and tiny polished sea shells. Her hair was freshly shampooed and held back from her face with a pearl clip, and she walked in a faint cloud of scent with a soft undertone of moss and roses. Her smile as she met Andrea's eyes was rueful, since she knew she had never looked better in her life.

"Ravishing," he said with what appeared to be warm, even heated, appreciation in the darkness of his eyes. "This is good, what I ordered, no?"

"This is good, yes," she said, then clicked her tongue in exasperation for how easily she had followed his lead. "I mean no! It's not good. It's too much."

He shrugged. "For a woman such as you, there is no such thing."

"If you are saying I asked for more than I—"

"No, no. You did not ask for enough." He moved to pour the ruby-colored wine that waited on a side table. Turning to hand her a glass, he went on. "I only meant to say you deserve whatever there is, and far more besides."

"I don't know how you figure that."

He glanced down at Guaio that had glided into the room behind her and was now winding around her ankles. "You prevented our friend here from becoming lost in the fog, which in turn saved me from annihilation by Bella. You have endured all manner of frights and inconveniences without hysterics. Providing a few items for your comfort is the least I can do."

How could she argue with that? She'd only wind up sounding as if she wanted more assurances or, heaven forbid, compliments. She sipped her wine, hoping that would help conceal the flush that burned its way to her hairline.

Dinner was a sumptuous meal that began with delicately flavored vegetable pasta and artichoke salad, continued with veal scaloppini and ended with cheese and fresh fruit. A different wine was served with each course, all of them equally delicious.

Dana was not used to wine at dinner, so was wary of the effect. She need not have worried. The relaxed pace of the meal prevented any sense of intoxication. She felt pampered, mellow and slightly euphoric, instead, though she suspected it was the company more than the wine that caused the last. That she was on a private island, the guest of a ridiculously wealthy Italian who thought she was in danger was like a dream. She would wake up soon and have a good laugh at her weird imagination.

Adding to the surreal effect was the presence of Guaio at the table. Well, or rather the closest thing to it since he had his own small table of gold-plated metal with a pair of ceramic bowls inset into the surface, one holding bottled water and the other cat food that appeared to be topped with caviar.

Despite this elegant dining accommodation placed between Andrea's chair and her own, the cat seemed to prefer bits of veal from the table above him. He demanded them in querulous tones and Dana obliged, partly for the fun of watching him accept her offering while ignoring those from Andrea, but also because feeding him helped ease the awkwardness that lingered between them.

"You will spoil him," Andrea observed, watching her slip Guaio a bit of brie from the dessert board that also held raspberries and sliced peaches.

Dana looked up with a laugh. "You have got to be kidding."

"Hand-feeding him? Allowing him to con you into sharing half your meal?"

"He looks to me as if he's quite used to it."

He tipped his head. "With Bella only."

She thought for an instant he meant he had no intention of pandering to a cat. That was before she caught the grim look on his face. "Not with her husband? I thought you said they were fighting over him."

"No affection comes into it, if that's what you think. The truth is Rico is jealous of Guaio. I did tell you Bella fears he will do away with him."

"It still seems unbelievable."

"People do strange things when involved in a divorce. Everything becomes a battle of wills and egos, and of making certain injury is returned for injury."

She gave him a straight look. "That sounds as if you speak from experience."

"I have never been married or divorced, if this is what you mean."

She shouldn't have said such a thing, but couldn't be sorry for it. She had the answer to a question that had bothered her from the minute they reached the island. "I didn't mean to pry."

"It doesn't matter," he said. "It was my parent's divorce years ago that I spoke of, also those of too many friends."

"I suppose it goes with the territory."

"Being Italian, you mean? I assure you divorce is no more frequent here than in the States."

She gave a quick shake of her head. "I only meant it seems to go with wealth. Building something together, working toward a better life for their children and each other, is never a necessity for those who have it. There is less likelihood, or so it seems, of becoming true partners, a couple facing their triumphs and failures, joys and sorrows together."

"And do you speak of this partnership from experience?" he asked, his eyes tightening at the corners.

"Only from the marriage of my parents, so far," she said with wry honesty.

"Then you are fortunate in having been brought up in a home with such harmony."

It was true enough, as Dana well knew. She had just never looked at it from quite that angle.

The meal came to an end. Andrea suggested a move into the living room for after-dinner coffee while Luisa cleared the dining table. As Dana rose and lead the way, he followed close behind her.

"You wear the perfume I ordered for you, I think," he said, his voice rich with satisfaction.

"I couldn't resist, though I should have."

"Most definitely you should not. It suits you perfectly, as I suspected it would."

He was so pleased with himself it was almost comical. He had good reason, but it was still a bit trying. "Of course, the bottle was rather small," she said with the faintest of shrugs.

"Was it?" A groove appeared between his eyes.

"Tiny. Hardly more than a sample."

He muttered an oath under his breath. Reaching into his pocket, he brought out his phone and began to thumb the screen.

"No!" She shot out her hand to snatch the cell phone

from his grasp.

"What are you doing?" He looked more surprised than angry, to the point that he made no attempt to regain his property.

"You are downright dangerous with this thing," she said, thumping it down on a table next to where they had come to a halt. "You don't need it right now."

"But I must take care of this problem."

She sighed, tried to control a smile and failed. "There is no problem, Andrea. Even I know an ounce of perfume comes in a small bottle."

"Not," he answered, "if I say otherwise. You may have a liter of this fragrance if you like it."

"A liter."

"Two liters. Or even a gallon."

"I don't need a drop more than I have already, okay? I was only teasing. Everything else was so over the top, except for this little one ounce bottle—"

"When I have my phone back, you will have enough to bathe in."

He was so serious, so arrogantly determined to please that she laughed with a quick shake of her head. "I don't think you'd like that, as you're the one who would have to endure the after-effects."

"Then again, *cara*," he said with an answering smile curling the finely molded lines of his mouth. "I can think of a situation where I might like it very much."

She suspected he was teasing her in his turn. The trouble was she could not be sure. He might also be bored with being stranded here, therefore ready for a mild flirtation to pass the time. They were alone, she was available, and he had, after all, gone to considerable expense to see that she was presentable.

"I don't believe I will wait for the coffee," she said abruptly. "I'm still rather tired in spite of my nap. I'll call it a night, if you don't mind."

"*Certo*," he said, sounding very Italian for the first time in hours. His gaze searched her face as if to verify her claim. "You have everything you need?"

"And then some." Wry humor threaded her voice.

"I will walk you to your room then."

"There's no need. I have my escort," She tipped her head toward Guaio who had followed them from the dining room and sat nearby, watching her every move with his intent blue stare.

She thought something very like disappointment flashed across Andrea face. If so, it was banished just as quickly, for his features reflected only the politeness of a host as he said goodnight.

Had leaving the company of an interesting man that way been prudent or merely foolish? Dana pondered that question long after she closed the door of her room behind her. Maybe she was giving herself too much credit by assuming her host might be coming on to her. There had been little outward sign earlier. He hadn't checked out her cleavage so obviously that she caught him at it; hadn't leered at her over his wine glass or tried to fondle her beneath the table.

Still, there had been something between them, a

constant zing of awareness that kept her on edge every moment she was around Andrea Tonello.

It could be she was the only one who felt it, of course. And what would that mean?

She couldn't sleep. Either because of that nap or the crazy circumstances she was in, she lay staring into the darkness, listening to the quiet creaks and pops of the old house and endless wash of the sea beyond her open window. The events of the day shifted through her mind over and over: the moment when the black sedan almost ran her down, the sight of her rental car plunging over the cliff, the way she had been tricked and brought here, and the moment when she and Andrea had been under fire out there on the headland. She felt as if she had endured a week of incredible happenings instead of a single day.

A cat was behind it all, or so Andrea said. How farfetched was that?

Yet Guaio was here, and he was obviously no ordinary feline. Would she have believed what Andrea told her otherwise? Would she have accepted the reason he gave for whisking her here to his island home, or only laughed in his face?

She could have slipped away this afternoon while he swam laps in the pool, or at least given it a good try. No one had been watching. She might have reached the harbor and either stowed away on a boat leaving for the mainland or stayed hidden until she could slip onto the ferry unseen.

There was a ferry she was certain, for she had watched it plow its way to the island and then leave again. What she didn't know was whether it ran every day or only once or twice per week.

She had no money, it was true, but it had crossed her mind that Andrea's wallet might have been left behind in the pool house. Though it would have gone against everything she had been taught or stood for, she could easily have made a quick detour to raid it.

Why hadn't she done any of that? Why had she simply closed her eyes and went to sleep there on the terrace?

A large part of it was her policewoman's certainty that she could take care of herself, thank you very much, while also making certain no crime was committed against man or beast. Beyond that was her ever-growing curiosity, the need to know exactly what was going on and how she figured into it. She was inclined to investigate a bit, really, to discover if everything was the way it had been explained to her.

She also needed to know if her life was actually in danger. The best way to discover that seemed to be to remain on the island. That should also allow her to find out how the fight over the cat ended.

All these things figured into her lack of action, yes. But was there something more?

She was no naive twenty-something, looking at this situation as a thrilling adventure complete with an Italian stud as rich as he was hot. That kind of spontaneity was not her usual response to anything.

She was no great believer in fate, either. Yet being here had a rightness that defied logic.

She was worried about her belongings, her liability for the rental car and the damage it had done to the guard rail. She hated leaving Suzanne and Caryn hanging at the rented villa, uncertain of where she was or what was happening to her. And yet she had no driving need to flee back to the mainland.

It was a conundrum that defied solution, no matter how hard she tried. When morning came, she had only lavender-blue circles under her eyes to show for her hours in bed.

Among the cosmetics sent on Andrea's orders was moisturizer that acted as light makeup and concealer. To that base she added peach lip gloss and brown mascara, and thought she managed to look halfway human. With her hair caught up in a ponytail held by a white elastic band, wearing white knee-length shorts with an aqua T-shirt with a woven neckline, she went in search of breakfast for herself and her faithful companion, Guaio.

The cat ran ahead of her down the stairs, his tail high and brown tip waving over his back. He didn't wait for her but continued along the downstairs hall in the direction of the kitchen. It seemed he might have a better idea of where to find food than she did.

In the end, however, she had only to follow the wonderful aromas of coffee and rolls warm from the oven. It led her through the wide French doors thrown open to the morning breeze and out onto the terrace.

Andrea looked up from the newspaper in front of him. A warm smile lighted his face. He folded the newsprint pages and laid them aside before rising to hold a chair for her.

"How are you this morning? You slept well?"

"I'm fine and I did," Dana replied, since her mother always said a guest never complained. It was only a small white lie, after all, as the fresh sea breeze and warmth of the sun were already lifting her spirits.

"Your shoulder is all right? No soreness or pain?"

She shook her head, saved from a fuller reply by the arrival of Tommaso bearing a tray with fresh coffee, a personal basket of rolls for her as well as dishes of butter, fresh fruit and yogurt. He gave her a cheery *buon giorno* as he set off the items. That done, he shook out her napkin and draped it over her lap before pouring hot coffee and milk for her. Her murmured thank you was met with a grin before he stood back with his tray at his side.

Andrea's nod of dismissal seemed to disappoint the boy. His footsteps were much slower as he departed than when he arrived.

Dana, glancing toward Andrea, caught him frowning after Tommaso. "What is it?"

He turned his gaze to her then reached for his coffee cup. "Nothing, nothing at all. Guaio came down with you just now?"

"He did, though he deserted me for the delights of the kitchen."

"You must not take it personally," he said, his face grave though amusement gleamed in his eyes. "His litter box is in the laundry beyond it. Also his food as Luisa usually feeds him."

"He has been here before then." She broke open one of

the warm, crusty rolls, dabbed it with butter and took a small bite.

"On many occasions with Bella. Until this year, she and Rico often spent their August holidays here on the island."

As Dana sat there with the Mediterranean spread out before her and its breeze caressing her face, the European habit of retreating from cities and towns for a month of relaxation at the sea shore seemed a fine habit. "Bella won't be coming now?"

"Legal matters concerning the divorce have detained her in the city, though she may get away later."

"The city?" She sipped her *caffè e latte*, enjoying the mingling of its flavor with that of the freshly baked rolls.

"Naples. She and Rico have a house there, though he moved into an apartment a few weeks ago. She speaks of going to Rome as it will be a better center for her work. She designs knitting patterns for yarn companies."

"As a job, you mean?"

A smile came and went across his face. "Her work is very good, quite fashionable, but she has no need to support herself. It is more an art form than a job."

"I suppose so," Dana said shortly, while color seeped under her skin. "Where I come from, work is seldom an art."

"No, this I understand. Your life has been different."

She acknowledged the concept with a nod. "But I thought you said her husband accused her of turning Guaio into a champion show cat for the prize money."

"So I did. This is because he has never realized the

extent of her participation in our father's estate."

Dana stared at him for a long moment. "You mean your sister never told him?"

"He never asked, but assumed he was the wealthier of the two of them, the breadwinner, as you would say. She allowed him to think so."

"Good grief, it's no wonder they separated."

He lifted a dark brow. "Meaning?"

"How could they ever expect to be happy with so many secrets between them?"

"They are much in love—or were when they married. There was a time when they could not keep their hands off each other."

"But there's more to marriage than love and great sex. It's about sharing thoughts and feeling, goals and dreams. It's being certain, no matter what happens, that the other person always means only the best toward you."

He opened his mouth to answer, but then snapped it closed without a sound. Pushing back his coffee cup, he sprang to his feet and walked out to the edge of the terrace. He stood there, feet spread and hands at his waist, staring at the horizon where the sea met the sky.

In that same moment, Dana heard the humming noise that put him on alert. It was an aircraft, the sound of its engine rising as it came closer. She jumped to her feet and moved to Andrea's side. Lifting her hand to shade her eyes, she followed his gaze.

It was a small plane rather than a commercial air liner, a private twin engine job that appeared silver as it reflected the morning sunlight. It was coming in fast, holding on a course that would take it directly over the island and the villa.

"They're too low," Dana said, almost to herself. "What are they doing?"

"Inside," Andrea rapped out in quiet command. "Go. Now."

She turned to him, but had no chance to question his meaning. He was already moving, wrapping a hard arm around her waist. He swept her with him back across the terrace, past their breakfast table under the pergola and into the villa. Just within the open door, he stopped and turned back to watch the plane with a scowl between his eyes.

It zoomed overhead, so near the ground that the wind of its passage set the palm trees at the end of the house to thrashing. The rattle of their fronds sounded like a rainstorm for an instant, then died away as the plane banked and turned, heading back toward the mainland.

"You think that was Rico's men again?"

The question was abrupt and just a little breathless as Dana spoke, partly from the quick run for cover, but also because she was standing in the protective circle of Andrea's arm. Her hip and thigh pressed against his so she felt the electric sting of nerve endings firing along their entire length, while the grasp of his hand at her waist had possessive heat and firmness.

"I don't know, but I intend to find out," he answered, turning his head to gaze down at her.

"It seems senseless, just buzzing the villa. What on earth was the purpose?"

"To discover if Bella is here, perhaps. Or if you are still with me after what took place yesterday afternoon."

"The pilot saw us, I think." She could see herself reflected in his eyes, see the way his pupils darkened, dilating with the dimness here compared to the outside brightness, or perhaps with something more.

"Probably."

"So now he knows. And Rico will know."

Andrea smiled, a slow and sensual movement of his mouth that held absolutely no humor. "*Certo, cara.* Now he will."

Six

"A re you sure it couldn't have been something else," Dana asked, her eyes like dark pools as Andrea gazed down at her. "I mean, you haven't placed an order that was to be airlifted and dropped off?"

"Such as?" He knew he'd done no such thing, but wanted to see what she would say.

"How should I know? I'm not a billionaire with people waiting at my beck and call."

She put a hand on his chest and gave a slight push as she spoke. He ignored the hint that she would like to be released. The feel of her against him was too beguiling, too perfect to be ended before it was absolutely necessary. "I suspect there are those who would come if you called them."

"Which has nothing to do with the fact that someone may have been spying on us!"

He enjoyed her attempts to be practical and severe almost as much as the soft color that spread over her cheekbones at such times. He was also enthralled by the soft curves that he could feel against his arm where he held her.

"Don't disturb yourself, *cara*," he said. "I have ordered nothing, but we are in no danger."

"So you say."

"I do, at least for now." He released her, though his muscles knotted with reluctance before they obeyed him. "But I think I must call Bella. I had intended to go today to Naples to see her, to discover what she may know about what's happening. I would rather not do that now."

"You think the plane may come back?"

"I prefer to take no chances."

She gave him a frown. "You think it might land—but I don't remember seeing an airstrip."

"It's on the far side of the island where the terrain is more suitable."

She gazed at him for a moment as if he had grown two heads. He fully expected her to ask if he kept a plane there, but she did not.

"My father built it," he said in answer to the question in her eyes. "It was trendy at the time, having a private plane and airstrip. For myself, I find the chopper more convenient."

"Oh, well, it's nice to have a choice."

He disregarded the flippant tone of that comment, answering as if she had been perfectly serious. "*Si, certo.*"

Andrea might have sought privacy for the call to Bella, but that meant leaving Dana alone after what had just happened. He didn't believe she was really upset, but he wanted to keep her in sight. That was merely the act of a careful host, of course. There was nothing else to it whatever.

He took out his phone retrieved last night from the table where Dana had left it. Avoiding her gaze, he thumbed in the number for his sister.

Bella was just as horrified as might be expected to hear what had been happening; her cries of shock and outrage made him jerk the phone away from his ear. That Dana could hear every word out of his sister's mouth went without saying. Though she might not understand entirely, or be familiar with the uncomplimentary names Bella applied to her husband, the gist of it was surely recognizable.

"But what is this of an American woman. Andrea?" his sister demanded. "Tell me again why she is there with you. Is she most beautiful? Have you begun an affair with her?"

"No and no," he said firmly. "I told you it's a matter of her safety."

"So you did. Yet I am astonished that you would take her with you to the island. This is a place for family, not for flirtations with a tourist. This is not like you, Andrea, not like you at all."

"I would not have needed to bring her here except for Rico."

"He is being a donkey's behind in Armani. I am out of patience with him, and so I shall tell him when I see him again. As for threatening my precious pet, I will chop off Rico's favorite dangly bits if he harms a single whisker.

Truly, I am so furious with him I am beside myself!"

"*Si*, I can tell," Andrea said, his voice dry as he watched Dana's face to see if she had caught even a portion of this particular exchange. "But you will talk to him to see what he has been doing?"

"You may be sure! And if I discover he has hired these thick-headed cretins to come after you, I will not be responsible for what I say or do!"

"I'm not worried about them coming after me," Andrea said as forcefully as he was able. "What Rico must understand is that Dana has no part in this. She is not to be touched or menaced in any way. If it continues, it is I who will not be responsible for my actions."

"Andrea, such passion! What has happened to you? Perhaps I should come to the island and see for myself."

"You will be disappointed. What you must do, my dear sister, is talk to your husband, make peace with him before someone gets hurt."

There was more in the same vein, but Andrea cut it off at last. Repeating his command, he ended the call. He stood weighing the phone in his hand for a moment before putting it away.

Dana had walked away a bit to give him privacy. She said nothing when he turned to her, but stood hugging her arms around her as if chilled. The brown of her eyes was clear, the gray ring around the irises like small portals into her mind. She felt out of place, he suspected, in a country where she did not know the language, could not be expected to accept or understand volatile relationships full of fury and noise such as that between his sister and Rico.

Dana appeared all calm logic on the surface, confident within herself, admirably steadfast in her belief about the partnership and dedication of marriage. He honored her for these things. She also seemed to know little about the burning needs and jealousies, the fears and resentments that could flare into violence between some couples. The fierce consummation of body and spirit that could blend souls seemed foreign to her.

He suspected her serenity was on the surface only. She was more like the ancient volcano that brooded over the Bay of Naples, peaceful on the outside but with a fiery cauldron deep within. Such repressed needs and desires could build slowly, slowly until they were impossible to contain. It would be a lucky man who held her in his arms when their power was released.

"Your shoulder," he said, his voice unaccountably husky before he cleared his throat, "you changed the bandage this morning?"

She shook her head. "It's a bit awkward with one hand. I did try to keep it dry while I showered."

"*Permesso*, permit me, if you will." He stepped closer to slide his fingers under the short sleeve of her T-shirt and push it higher. The knit was so fine and soft that it was easily moved out of the way. She jerked a little at his first touch, but he didn't think it was because he hurt her. He was sure of it when she flushed and kept her gaze turned away from what he was doing.

As carefully as possible, he peeled away the adhesive

edges that held the bandage in place. The scratches appeared to be healing well, were already less red and angry looking than they had been the day before.

"Will I live?" she inquired with more than a little tartness.

"I believe so, though this bandage will need changing tonight." He smoothed it back into place, holding her arm as he secured the edges again.

"I'm sure I can manage." Her hair shifted on her shoulders like auburn silk as she turned to meet his gaze.

"But why should you, when I am here?" On an impulse he made no attempt to deny, Andrea bent his head and pressed his lips to the bandaged surface.

When he straightened again, she was watching him with her lips parted and an odd, suspended look in her eyes. For long seconds, neither of them moved or breathed. He could see the russet shading of her lashes under the light layer of her mascara, the fine grain of her skin, the scattered ghost of freckles under her sheer makeup. The scent he had given her, subtle and fresh as a spring woodland yet delicately floral, was enhanced by her own unique fragrance. It made him want to step closer, to gather her against him and lose himself in her for the rest of the day.

His hand on her arm tightened a fraction as he fought the urge. Her lashes came down and she removed herself from his grasp with a quick twist. "You should patent your bedside manner. You could make another fortune for yourself."

"Do you think so? It's a pleasure to know you appreciate it."

"I didn't say—"

"But I think you did, *cara*. Though I must tell you I prefer to keep my patient list exclusive and—intimate."

She gave a choked laugh. "You are so full of it."

The need to show her exactly how intimate he wished to be was so strong his eyes watered with it, and with the drawing pain in the lower part of his body. It was all he could do not to snatch her close and press his mouth to hers, sliding his tongue between her parted lips to savor the warm sweetness of her. Would she respond or remove herself from his grasp yet again? He would give a lot to know.

She was his guest, and a reluctant one at that. They had been through much together in a short time, but he was still a stranger to her. It would be wrong to take advantage of his position to start something between them, no matter how much his body applauded the idea. Besides, he preferred the women he took into his arms to be willing, even enthusiastic, participants.

"And you are so easy to tease that it's irresistible," he answered before turning away from her. "But it appears our visitor may have flown away for good. We could, if you like, go down and bathe in the sea."

"And that will be just lovely, playing in water where gun-toting idiots in a boat can plow right over us without any trouble."

"The cove below the villa is not only private but concealed from all but a direct approach. It's unlikely anyone will know we are there. And if they should discover it, we will have ample time to see them coming."

"You're sure?"

"You will enjoy the sea, and a little sun can be beneficial," he said in persuasive tones. "A half-hour or hour will
provide Vitamin D as well as giving you the nice beginnings
of a tan."

The look she gave him was skeptical. "I don't tan, I
promise you. I freckle. Besides, I have no swimsuit."

"Was there none among the things delivered?"

"Oh, yes, if you can call it that. The thing is so tiny I
thought for a minute it was a hair tie."

A corner of his mouth twitched. "You don't mean it."

"It looks more like something a pole dancer might
wear."

"A pole dancer."

"You aren't going to pretend you don't know what that
is?"

"No, no. I was just having trouble with the image." This
was true, though it was a vision of Dana dancing for him
alone that derailed his brain for an instant.

"Just think of a barely-there bikini that leaves nothing
whatever to the imagination, particularly in the rear."

She was going to kill him with this image. If he didn't
lighten it somehow, he would embarrass them both with his
reaction. "I'm not sure I can visualize this," he said knotting
his brow for maximum effect. "Perhaps you could model it
for me."

"In. Your. Dreams."

"But it has a matching cover-up, yes?"

"You did order it, I knew it!"

His answer was a shrug. Why deny the obvious?

"Well, if you think I'm frolicking in the sea in three tiny triangles held together with dental floss, you are mistaken.

"But no one will be around to see."

"You will be there."

Yes, he would. He would indeed, though he was suddenly disinclined to have any other man witness this spectacle. Tommaso, for instance, who was so intrigued by their American guest he found excuses to serve her, or the gardeners who had appeared on the terrace to sweep and water plants more often in the past twenty-four hours than in the whole previous month.

Modesty could actually be an endearing trait, he discovered in some surprise. Reaching into his pocket, he pulled out his cell phone. "You would prefer a maillot, I believe. What color?"

"Put that thing away," she said in exasperation, batting it out of reach of his poised finger. "Didn't you tell me there are extra suits in the pool house? Surely there's something that will do."

Practicality in a woman also had its appeal.

The sea was perfect; calm, extravagantly blue, with sunlight glinting on its surface like a sprinkling of diamond dust. Andrea carried their beach equipment under one arm while giving Dana his hand as they descended the stone steps cut into the hillside below the terrace. It was just as well he had a good grip on her, as she stumbled twice, being more interested in watching the sea than looking where she was going.

"No one is anywhere around, I promise," he said as he handed her around a rock outcropping that made the path slant even as it concealed the cove from the house.

She gave him a smiling, upward glance. "Oh, I believe you. It's just that it's so beautiful here, so close to how I imagined an Italian seaside would be."

It was so unlike the usual crowded beach that he blinked but did not bother to correct her. "I am sorry it hasn't been a better holiday for you. Perhaps an extension can be arranged."

"I doubt it," she said with a small shake of her head.

"You must return soon then. If you like, I can—"

"I'm sure you could. But it's okay, really, it is. I'll rejoin my friends soon, and everything will be fine."

She was looking forward to getting off the island, getting away to enjoy Positano as planned. Andrea could hardly blame her, but he didn't have to like it.

Nor did he care for the extra reminder that her time here was limited. The sooner the business with Rico was cleared away, the sooner he would have to let her go. That was unless he could arrange matters so she would have to stay.

The cove was a stretch of cream-colored sand that backed onto a low cliff and was enclosed by arm-like ramparts of rock on either side. The waves that washed into it were clear, gentle and rhythmic. They whispered onto the sand and lapped over and around the outcroppings of rock that dotted the shoreline, forming small hollows that trapped sand, bits of shells and small sea creatures. Andrea stood for a moment with his fists on his hips, watching, listening.

Nothing moved except a few gulls and a freighter far out to sea, a square, slow-moving ship small with distance. There was no sound except the wind and waves. They were alone, their privacy complete.

He spread a blanket over the sand. Dana settled onto it on her knees, setting out the sunglasses, sunscreen, and chilled drinks and snacks from the beach bag. While she was busy with that, he erected a large beach umbrella for shade.

The maillot she'd chosen from the pool house collection was black with a honey-colored diagonal slash across the front. If she'd expected an Italian-made suit to be utilitarian, however, she had miscalculated. The slash emphasized her narrow waist, while the neckline and back plunged to breath-taking depths and the leg openings reached dazzling heights. She might have been less covered in the bikini, Andrea saw with pleasure from his height above her, but she could hardly have been more provocative.

Sea-bathing was going to be one of his better ideas. He was sure of it.

~ ~ ~

Dana felt as if she could sit and look at the Mediterranean for hours. Just breathing the air that swept toward her, knowing it blew from exotic places like Sicily and Corsica and Africa, was reward enough, but to do it in such quiet privacy was priceless. She could feel the tension seep from her neck and shoulders, sense the kinks in her brain unwinding.

It was unlikely she would have enjoyed this kind of peace in Positano with Caryn and Suzanne. It seemed disloyal to her friends to think such a thing, but it was true. Even if they could have found a beach as protected as this one, Suzanne would have chattered about everything under the sun while playing heavy metal at top volume. Caryn would have insisted on moving the blanket at least three times already, in search of the perfect sand, perfect spot to get the perfect tan. The pair of them was great fun, and she loved them, but couldn't call them restful companions.

Andrea was different. Though alert for anything that might disturb this beach idyll, he had an enviable air of being at ease within himself, and completely present in the pleasure of the moment. Better than that, he didn't hover, but had the consideration to take himself off for a swim after a time, allowing her to bask in the sun without an audience. She could see his dark head and strong shoulders as he powered through the waves with effortless ease, looking as at home in the water as on the land.

He was heading out to sea, or so it seemed. Already, he was beyond the rocky arms of the enclosure. Was he only testing his limit, or could he be seeking open water to make certain no intruders were lurking on this side of the island?

His head vanished beneath a wave. When it did not immediately reappear, Dana got to her feet, shading her eyes as she focused on the distant waves. A hollow feeling settled in her chest when she still couldn't see him. She moved off the blanket, took a step closer to the water.

Oh, there he was, swimming in the opposite direction but parallel to the shoreline. He must have dived and then changed directions.

He was still drawing away from her. His head was no more than a black dot now, one that came and went with the wave action. Keeping it in view as best she could, Dana walked toward the water.

The quiet surge of the sea around her feet was cool and inviting. There was no heavy surf like that of the Florida panhandle where her family had always gone on family vacations. The water here was more seductive, enticing her so she waded out until it reached above her ankles, her knees, and then her thighs.

A moment later, she struck out, swimming toward where she had last seen Andrea. It felt so good, that buoyant gliding through the water, the flow of it around her, over her, under her. The lift of the salt water was different from the pool at the gym where she worked out after work. Swimming had been her exercise of choice since the days of competing with her high school swim team. For long minutes it almost felt as if she could swim forever.

It wouldn't do. She didn't know the coast, had no idea of its tides or rip currents. Besides, it wasn't too smart to put too much distance between her and the cove; she had passed out of its enclosing arms moments ago.

Turning to her back, she floated a few seconds to rest and get her bearings. Then she reversed her direction, heading back toward the cove.

"You are okay?"

She hadn't heard Andrea's approach, yet there he was beside her. She controlled a start, even as she breathed deep on her forward stroke. "I'm fine."

"Excellent. I'm glad you came into the water. I thought perhaps you would sunbathe only."

Darn a man who could talk and swim as if it were nothing, and that after swimming halfway to the mainland before coming back to join her. She was in fair shape, but he definitely had more stamina. "Now you know why I wanted a maillot."

"I will change the bandage on your shoulder when we have dried off."

"Good." She couldn't fault his attentiveness as a host anyway.

He seemed to take the hint at that short answer, for he didn't speak again. Neither did he outdistance her though she was well aware it would have been easy for him. He matched his pace to hers with deliberate restraint, swimming shoulder to shoulder through the blue, blue waters toward the crescent cove that waited for them.

The water turned shallow. Dana pushed to her feet with Andrea at her side.

Her foot came down on a bit of a broken shell. Before it could cut into her, she shifted her weight, but then staggered a little as a shallow wave caught her off balance.

Instantly, he steadied her with an arm about her waist. Then he swooped to place his other arm behind her knees. Lifting her against his chest, he strode with her toward the beach.

"I can walk," she protested. "I just stepped on something."

"You may be tired. I'm not."

"You're a show-off."

She might not have sounded so peevish, except she was too aware of the corded muscles of his arms that held her, his bare chest against her, and the thinness of the wet fabric that prevented the rub of his bare skin against hers. Also of the shivery excitement these things touched off inside her.

He grinned down at her. "This could be, I will admit it."

Dear heaven, but he was something to look at with his green eyes reflecting light from the sea, his lashes in black spikes, teeth flashing white in the sun-burnished olive of his face and dark hair curling onto his forehead, dripping water that ran down the straight line of his nose.

Dana felt something turn over deep inside her with recognition that was almost like pain. And she realized with conscious irony that if she had to be abducted, she was lucky the man responsible was Andrea Tonello.

Back on the blanket once more, they pulled bottled water from the beach bag and chased the salt water taste from their mouths. Then her ever-considerate host set his bottle aside and eased closer, reaching to peel away the wet bandage from her shoulder, apparently intent on replacing it with a new one.

The touch of his fingers sent such tingles radiating through her nerve endings that Dana rushed into speech. "I shouldn't have gone into the water, I expect. I wasn't thinking, actually forgot about the scratches."

"It doesn't matter," he answered as he worked. "Salt water has a healing effect. This was discovered long ago by sailors who saw wounds got well sooner while they were at sea."

"You're just trying to make me feel better."

"Would I do that?"

"If you thought it would help." She sent him a glance over her shoulder.

"And is it?"

The warm vein of humor in his voice did strange things inside her. "Maybe. Anyway, you're just full of information, aren't you?"

"As well as BS?" he asked with astringency as he peeled open a new bandage package that he took from the endless depths of the beach bag.

"I never said that."

"Not precisely, but it's what you meant."

Maybe she had, at that. She wondered if her comment had actually bothered him, or if he was only reminding her of how she had judged him before. "Well, you only have yourself to blame."

"Yes."

He smoothed over the bandage edges to make sure they stuck, but didn't kiss it to make it well this time. It seemed the salt water was going to have to do the trick all by itself.

Not that she was disappointed, or so Dana told herself. Certainly not.

Picking up the wet bandage and pieces of wrapper,

Andrea tucked them into her hand. "If you will put that in the trash bag and hand me the sunscreen, I'll put it on for you." He reached to reset the beach umbrella, angling it so she was more fully protected by its shade as he spoke over his shoulder. "You've had enough sun for one day, I think."

He was right, she knew. She was aware of a slight warning sting on the tops of her shoulders, could almost feel the freckles popping out beneath. Groping in the beach bag, she found the sunscreen tube and handed it to him. She turned her back, braced herself and waited.

His touch was firm and sure, with no hesitation in it at all. He smoothed the cream lightly over one shoulder and then across to the other before spreading it down her back. The depth he could reach was a reminder of the low cut of her suit. It left her some mystery back there, she knew, but not a lot.

His movements slowed, stopped. His voice sounded strained as he spoke. "You have a tattoo."

"No!" she said in pretended amazement.

"Most of it is covered so I can't quite see the design. May I?"

This was a little like asking if he could look at her backside, though the inked drawing was actually in the small of her back. Putting a hand behind her, she lowered the dip of the suit to expose what she thought was most of the design. At least that way she could control how much of her he could see.

"A boy on a dolphin." The words were soft, almost contemplative.

"Actually, a girl on a dolphin," she corrected. "If you look close enough, you'll see she has breasts and long hair."

"I do see. And it means—what?" He eased her hand aside and pulled the edge of the suit back up. A second later, he began to spread sunscreen again.

"I was on the swim team at school, for one thing. More than that, our family used to go to the beach every summer. I loved the sea when I first saw it, love it still."

"Yet you live in Atlanta, which is landlocked, I believe."

"We don't always get to choose where we live."

"Have you never thought of moving?"

She gave a soft laugh. "Many times, really. One year we rented a beach house that had a plaque on the wall that said it all."

"Yes?"

Keeping her voice light, almost whimsical, she quoted:

"Of all the things that life can bring,
I ask for only three:
bread for my need, books to read,
and a house beside the sea."

"Ah, *certo*. Then you must have this house," he said with assurance.

"If only it was that easy!"

He touched her shoulder, turning her to face him. The expression in his eyes was serious as they met hers. "But it is easy, truly, if this is your desire."

She wanted to believe him. She really did, especially in that moment.

Though her ambition in the past had never reached

further than a condo beside the gulf where she had spent her summers, she suddenly longed to live beside the Mediterranean in a villa with thick stone walls where white curtains billowed in the sea breeze and the air was scented with brine and herbs. She wanted to watch the sun rise and set over the water from a 360-degree view, to hear the gulls cry and watch the distant water traffic passing by.

But she didn't want to live there alone. She wanted someone to talk to and laugh with and sleep close to at night, wrapped in loving, protective arms.

How stupid was that?

"Has no one ever told you this before?" he asked. "Did they never say that you must follow your heart to whatever makes you happy?"

She gave a small shake of her head. Her parents and her brothers loved her and wanted her near them. That meant in Atlanta. To them, the beach was a place to go and play but leave behind when they'd had enough sand and sun.

They thought life was supposed to be settled, with small ambitions and no dreams of things beyond reach. They could never understand, as Andrea had in an instant, the silent longings of the heart for something different, something permanent and beautiful within the sound of sea waves.

They hadn't understood at all why she had opted for a vacation on the Amalfi Coast when there was a perfectly good sugar-white sand coast only a few hours away.

Andrea eased forward to sit beside her with one knee drawn up and his wrist resting upon it while the sunscreen tube hung forgotten from his fingers.

"How is it you became a policewoman? Was this also something you desired?"

"It was, or at least I thought it was." She looked down, noticed a loose thread on the blanket where she was sitting and began to roll it in her fingers to prevent raveling. "My dad was a cop who worked his way up to detective, one of my brothers was on a fast track to join him, and the other was with the state police. It was the job I'd heard about all my life."

"You enjoy what you do, now you have joined them?"

"At times, when I can make a difference. I like being able to keep a drunk driver off the road or stay with someone injured in a wreck until the EMTs arrive, particularly a child or an older person."

He inclined his head in understanding. "And do you want to be a detective, too?

"I suppose. It has its appeal, solving the puzzle, finding justice for victims."

"That doesn't sound especially dedicated. Do you never think of doing anything different, of having a home and a family?"

"Sometimes, not that it matters." She lifted her head to meet his gaze head-on. "Can we talk of something else? This can't be interesting to you."

"But it is of great interest. I would like to know every-thing about you."

He sounded sincere, but that could come from nothing but boredom. At least it gave her an excuse to exercise her own curiosity. "Fine, but I get to ask you something for every question I answer."

"This is fair. What do you wish to know?"

"Asking about my family plans seem a little odd when you're living the bachelor life. Do you have none in that direction?"

"I would not say I have plans," he answered with a shift of one shoulder. "But I have come to an age when being without close ties is—unsatisfactory. I think now and then of having someone who cares whether I come home at night, also to join with in arranging a future that might include children."

The deep timbre of his voice and the things he'd said set off a quiet ache inside her. His view of what a marriage should be was not wildly exciting, perhaps, but had deep, sure purpose and intimations of permanence that carried its own appeal.

"You've arrived at this point at the great age of what— thirty? Thirty-five?" she asked.

"Thirty-four. And you have how many years?"

She could hardly refuse to answer since he'd been so forthcoming. "Twenty-seven, almost twenty-eight."

"It is strange that you are still free. The men you know must be idiots."

"Pretty much," she said on a laugh. "Actually I was engaged once, but discovered his ideas about what a wife should be and do were different from mine."

"Different how?"

"I was to stop working immediately after the wedding,

for a start. He would give me a household allowance, but no direct access to the family bank account. He would make the decisions on all major purchases. He expected three freshly cooked meals every day, and both lunch and dinner were to be on the table, waiting for him, when he came home for them. He would decide when and if we had friends over, when we went out and where we went on vacations. And it went downhill from there."

"He wished to control your lives together, and you."

"I suppose. He just picked the wrong woman."

"This fiancé sounds much like Rico, the kind to rant and rave when things fail to go his way. He was unhappy about the broken engagement, I expect, made much noise and many attempts to change your mind?"

"Good guess," she told him in some surprise. "He tried everything, even threats. That was, until my brothers put on their uniforms and paid him a visit."

He gave a low chuckle. "Good for them. Maybe we should ask your brothers to come have a talk with Rico."

"I thought of it, believe me—or at least thought of calling them."

His expression turned droll. "To talk to me, yes, as you said before. What changed your mind?"

"Two men in a boat," she said succinctly. "Well, and the fact that I haven't yet wound up duct-taped to a chair in your basement."

"I have no basement," he said with mock severity.

"Wine cellar then. Don't tell me you don't have one of those."

"*Certo*, this I have." He sighed. "Though I don't imagine you would stay in it for long, even tied to a chair."

"Not on your life." She paused. "Is it my turn again?"

"I've no idea, but it can be if you like." He inclined his head with the utmost politeness.

"Why don't you go talk to Rico? He deserves to hear a few home truths if he's the kind of dangerous bully he seems. I'd think you could put the fear of God into him if you felt like it."

"I would like nothing better," he said, looking away from her. "But it isn't that easy."

"Why ever not?"

"A marriage is an agreement between two people. The fewer who interfere when there is trouble, the better things may turn out for them, at least in most cases. Then I know very well Bella is not the easiest woman with which to live."

"So you're saying the problem between her and Rico is not all one-sided."

"Such things seldom are, I think. My sister is extravagant, as she had little reason to be frugal before her marriage. She thrives on excitement, travel, parties, learning and doing new things, especially meeting new people. Rico would like to spend his free time drinking beer and espresso with his friends and following World Cup games, sometimes with travel but most often in his big home media center."

"I would guess Bella isn't fond of soccer."

"Or television. She much prefers the theater, ballet, opera, museums, and so on. Her idea of entertainment is attending *La Scala*."

Dana gave him a quizzical look. "What on earth ever made them get married?"

"The attraction of opposites, I surmise. That and what Bella would probably call a grand passion."

"That part where they couldn't keep their hands off each other," she said with wry remembrance of his earlier description.

"Would that be a question? If so, it must be my turn now."

She waved a hand. "Ask away."

"You were never tempted again after this engagement, never found another man you thought it possible to marry?"

She shook her head. "I went to the police academy not long afterward. You'd think that would allow plenty of opportunities for meeting a man with a similar background and so on, but it didn't work that way. The atmosphere was—strained. A few of the guys thought it was cute that I wanted to carry a gun and take down the bad guys. The rest just wanted to see how badly I wanted the job, how much I could stand before I was so intimidated or grossed out that I quit.'"

She had endured the condescension, sabotage and crude practical jokes, and shown her mettle by coming out among the top ten in her class. She'd never spoken of the difficulty of it, however. Telling her father or her brothers would have gained their support, but forever marked her as a stoolie and a wimp who couldn't hack it, a female officer who had to call in males for backup. She'd have died first.

She'd thought she was tough after growing up with her two brothers in a predominantly male household where manners weren't exactly refined. She had been, compared to some of the female recruits. But she'd been tougher by the time she graduated.

Relating the circumstance to Andrea was different, somehow. He lived on the other side of the ocean, for one thing, so could never interfere. He was also more interested in how she felt about it than in wreaking vengeance for her sake.

At least, that was what she thought at first. The grim implacability that settled over his face could have another interpretation.

"It was better after you began to work at your job?"

That was two questions for his turn, but she let him get away with it since the subject was the same. "Somewhat," she agreed. "But my superior is scared to death I'll be killed on his watch, so creating a huge media headache and reams of paperwork for him. The most exciting thing I get to do is work accidents and chase down little old ladies late for bingo so going sixty miles an hour in a thirty mile zone."

"Not quite as exciting as bringing down the bad guys."

She looked away from the wry sympathy in his eyes. "What about you? Do you enjoy building ships, or whatever it is you do to add to the bottom line?"

"The shipyard was sold and moved to Naples two decades ago. Now I sit on the board of the company that bought it, also on those for a number of charitable foundations. On weekends, I work on a fifty-foot sail boat—a yacht you'd probably call it—building it from scratch."

"Really?"

He gave a light shrug. "It feels good to work with my hands. More than that, it's in the blood."

"That's the meaning behind this then?" She touched the gold signet ring on his finger with a fingertip, smoothing over its bas relief of a sailing ship.

He gave it a brief glance, as if he had forgotten he wore it. "It belonged to my great-grandfather who worked side-by-side with the men who were constructing his ships."

"You don't have to justify manual labor to me. I think it's grand that you can build something useful."

He chuckled. "I don't know how useful it's going to be."

"This boat will be seaworthy and get you where you want to go, right?"

"So I hope."

"Then it's useful. And no, that can't be counted as one of my questions!" she added as he looked on the point of doing that.

"I was only going to say the tops of your knees are turning red, which means I am failing in my job."

He sat up straighter and squeezed a generous amount of the sunscreen from the tube he still held. Dropping it, he rubbed his palms together to spread the cream over them. Without hesitation, he put his hands on her leg below her right knee and then swept them upward.

The sensation that surged along the path of his hands was stunning in its force. The nerves of her leg jumped with it, fluttering with vibrations she felt deep in her body as he inched steadily higher, over her knee, up her thigh.

She inhaled in sharp surprise and clamped her hands on his wrists.

His movements stilled, but he did not take his hands away. He met her gaze, his own darkly green there under the umbrella's shadow.

Neither of them moved for endless seconds while the sand shimmered around them and the breeze off the water stirred their hair. Dana barely breathed. Anticipation hovered inside her along with the warring urges to invite him closer and also to push him away.

She hadn't set out to have a holiday affair of the kind she and Caryn and Suzanne had joked about. It just wasn't her style. She was also too wary of the kind of men who might think it a fine joke to give an American tourist a thrill.

Andrea wasn't like that.

He was at the other end of the spectrum, if anything: upper class and beyond wealthy, a fantasy man, impossibly handsome, dynamic, cultured, strong and accomplished. He was far too amazing for anything permanent to come from an affair with a garden variety cop's daughter. Still, there was this moment.

She lowered her gaze, allowing it to settle on his mouth. His lips were parted as if his breathing was as shallow as hers. As she watched, he leaned toward her, and then hesitated.

Without conscious thought, she released her grip on his wrists. She lifted a hand to place her fingertips on the warm, firm muscles of his chest, trailing them down to where his heartbeat shuddered against his breastbone. Her lips tingled as if with the rush of the hot blood she could feel surging through her veins, pooling in her lower body. She inclined her head toward his in a minute movement.

"*Dio*," he whispered, and slid one arm around her waist, drawing her to him before settling his mouth upon hers.

He tasted of heat and power and sea salt, with an underlying sweetness that was her undoing. She opened to him, needing more, wanting to mingle her essence with his as their tongues meshed and stroked. She shifted her grasp to his shoulder, drawing him closer before sliding her fingers into his hair and closing them on its dark, crisp silk. Mindless in a single instant, she clung as she felt him lower her to the blanket, sensed its warmth and softness against her back. Her only concern, a vague fear in the back of her mind, was that he would break the connection between them.

He did not.

Supporting himself on one elbow, he plumbed the depths of her mouth, flicking the satin surfaces with his tongue, gliding along the chiseled edges of her teeth. At the same time, he placed his hand on her ribcage covered by her damp suit, spanning it, learning it, before moving upward to cup her breast.

She made a low sound in her throat as he enclosed that soft mound in his grasp, gently encompassing before brushing his thumb over its apex. She felt her nipple bead, felt a drawing sensation inside as it elongated as if seeking more of his touch.

Andrea turned his head, his breathing harsh, irregular against her cheek. "I want you, *cara*," he said. "I want you, need you, more than life."

She could not have answered, even if she'd dared. She wanted him, too, but could see no future for them while they were of different continents, different worlds. Oh, but what did that matter while the sweep of his hand across her abdomen, the spread of his fingers over the mound at the tops of her thighs left her half delirious with longing, so weak with it she wanted nothing more than to hold him to her while the earth spun away to nothing.

He trailed kisses along the side of her face to the hollow behind her ear, and then down the curve of her neck to her collarbone. As she arched her neck to give him access, he licked along her shoulder, pressing kisses to it, taking small nips with his teeth.

She hardly knew when he returned his free hand to her cleavage, sliding his fingers into it and skimming upward to ease the damp strap of her suit from her shoulder. She gasped, arching into him as she felt the hot suction of his mouth on her nipple. Shivering, turning to twine her legs with his, pressing against his thigh, she held his head to her while her heart doubled its beat and pleasure exploded along her every nerve ending.

She brushed her hands over his back, reveling in the corded muscle she found there, absorbing the restrained power of him. .She wanted that inside her, yearned for it as she'd never yearned for anything in her life. The need for connection was so great that she pressed her mouth to his shoulder, the side of his neck, nudged his cheek until he turned his head and took her mouth again.

It was exactly what she wanted in that moment, but not enough, never enough. She moaned in distress, a sound that seemed to have an echo.

That sound didn't come from the man who held her.

It sprang from no great distance away, a low groaning that rose to a yowl and then became a high-pitched squall. It came closer, grew louder and more desperate. Like a lost soul's lament, it rent the air over and over.

Until it stopped.

Dana felt something probe her neck. Two furry feet rested upon her shoulder. Abruptly a warm damp nose touched her cheek, pushed between her forehead and that of the man who held her. A feline tongue rasped her cheek, then shifted to lick Andrea's chin.

He jerked with a whispered curse. Releasing her, he raised his head until he was nose to nose with Guaio.

Dana could not help smiling at the sight, though she felt dazed with unsatisfied need, uncertain whether to be glad or sorry for the interruption. All she knew was that being too well-liked by animals had its downside.

With every sign of reluctance then, Andrea reached to tug the strap of her suit back in place, covering her breast. He sat up, scrubbed his hands over his face and raked them back through his hair before giving a violent, full body shudder. He blinked as if waking from a trance.

He turned his head, then, and his mouth tugged in a slow and sardonic grin as he gazed down at the champion cat as it shifted to lie on her chest, purring in contentment.

He let out a sigh and glanced out to sea.

"I wonder," he said with a low growl in his voice, "if cats can swim."

SEVEN

A ndrea was not a devotee of nude beaches, had never paraded along one in naked nonchalance. He might have made love on a beach in his more heedless teenage years, but not since and never in broad daylight.

It wasn't that he'd grown prudish, but rather that he'd gained better sense. Long-range camera lenses made nonsense of pretension of seclusion, and he had no wish to see his backside displayed in the tabloids. No, nor to pay exorbitant sums to an enterprising paparazzo to keep it from their pages.

Beyond that, he respected his partners too much for such stupidity. He would not expose them to such needless embarrassment. At least, he never had before.

He had come close, so close, to making love to Dana under an open sky and with the sea murmuring at their feet. It was truly incredible.

The woman destroyed his ability to think in a way he

didn't understand. It had never happened to him before, this abandonment of principles he'd thought so embedded there was no need to think of them. She tempted him past his will to resist.

The irony of it was that she wasn't even trying.

God help him if she should ever decide to try.

He barely knew her, or she him. They had been through a number of precarious situations together, but closeness wasn't necessarily a by-product. Regardless, he was drawn to her like a thirsty man to cool water. He'd told her he wanted to know everything about her and meant just that. He wanted to know what she'd been like as a child, the things she'd done and seen that brought her joy, and how she felt on the issues of the moment.

Her skin enthralled him, its satiny sheen and pale, blue-veined smoothness where sun had never touched, also the tracing of golden freckles on her shoulders. He wanted to lick those freckles like bits of candy, taking their sweetness on the tip of his tongue. And her nipples, such an amazing clear pink and incredibly tender, responding to his slightest touch in a way that made him steel-hard just remembering it.

He would do well to forget. Dana might allow herself to be charmed for a short while, but common sense would soon reestablish itself. Home for her was in the States with her family. When this business with Bella was done, she would rejoin her friends for the rest of her holiday. Following that, she would return to Atlanta and the position for which she was trained, and never think about him or the

Isola delle Palme delle Tonellos again.

Andrea knew these things well. Accepting them was something else altogether.

He and Dana returned to the house with Guaio following along behind them. They showered and changed, after which he retreated to his office while she sat on the terrace with a magazine in her lap.

He thought she napped out there in the pergola's shade, but couldn't be sure. He could only see her head and shoulders as he stood back at an angle from his study window.

An insect was buzzing around her. It wasn't dangerous, he knew, but might disturb her rest. He wanted to go and chase it away, but could not be sure that was all he would do. Swinging away from the window, he shoved his hands deep into his pockets and walked back to his desk.

The day slipped away. Andrea was as industrious as he knew how to be, talking on the phone to colleagues, working at his computer and clearing his inbox. He took the golf cart to the village, seeing to matters there and lunching at the new restaurant near the harbor as an excuse to issue a warning about the trash situation. And all the while, he wondered what his guest was doing, whether she was having lunch inside or outside, and if she was pleased to be eating without him.

Twice, he placed calls to Bella, but she didn't answer or return them. She might be at the hairdresser, having her nails done or indulging in a spa treatment. Wherever it was, she seemed out of contact for the day.

Stymied there, he searched his contacts for Rico and

almost made that call. What stopped him was the niggling feeling that his brother-in-law might not be at fault. He had, for the most part, distanced himself from his father's less respectable associates; how likely was he to turn to them now? Moreover, for all his shouting and bombast, Rico had never seemed the kind to inflict bodily harm, particularly on a woman.

Dinnertime came at last. It was a strained meal with only sporadic conversation. Andrea could sense Dana's doubt and impatience, but there was little he could do about it. He discovered more of her childhood with pointed questions, and revealed something of his plans for the boat he building. She asked how and when he had learned to pilot the helicopter, and they compared oddly similar tastes in music. And all the while, the memory of what had almost happened on the beach lay between them like an awkward guest at the table.

It was a relief when the cheese and fruit tray appeared, signaling the end of the torment. Andrea could not even be sorry when Dana elected to retire to her room immediately afterward. Yet when he'd said goodnight and watched her climb the stairs to her bedroom with Guaio leaping at her heels, he had to clench his teeth and press his lips together to keep from calling her back.

~ ~ ~

"So. What are you going to do?"

It was the following day, her third on the island, when Dana put that question to him. They were having a light lunch of seafood salad and bread sticks with a crisp white wine as a concession to the hot, dry wind that rustled the grape leaves on the pergola above them.

"About what?" Andrea thought he knew, but felt it best to be clear.

"Rico and the threat he represents, of course. You can't just do nothing in the hope it will all go away."

That was exactly what he was doing in a sense. Things often did just go away if ignored, at least in Andrea's experience. That there had been no new menace in the past twenty-four hours and more suggested it might yet turn out that way.

"Are you so anxious to leave here then?"

She glanced past his shoulder, avoiding his eyes. "I can't stay forever."

"Unfortunately," he replied as lightly as he was able.

She colored a little. "That's nice of you, very hospitable, but unnecessary."

She seemed to think he was merely being polite or maybe flirtatious. "Dana—"

"You and I both know this is just a temporary thing. It will be over in a day or two and we will go our separate ways."

He did know it, which was one reason he was in no hurry to cause changes that might speed the parting. He could get used to sharing his meals with her, reaching to touch her now and then when he was able to manufacture an excuse. His sigh was silent before he spoke.

"I need to speak to Bella again, but can't reach her."

"You don't think something has happened to her?"

"I contacted her housekeeper. She was upset after we spoke on the phone, and has been in and out trying to catch up with Rico. Somehow, they keep missing each other."

"That's all very well, but things have been quiet for a while now. I can't just hang out here for no reason."

"What if they are only quiet because you are here with me?"

"Meaning something might happen if I leave? Oh, please!"

He hunched a shoulder. "It isn't impossible."

"It isn't likely, either, not if it's Guaio these people want."

"I told you—"

"They have no reason to think there's anything between us that would make me useful as a hostage!"

"None except what happened on the beach yesterday morning."

The pink shading to her features was his reward for bringing up that reminder, just as the effect on his body was his punishment.

"You're saying someone saw us?"

"Not that I know of, but it's possible."

Her eyes narrowed. "That's very convenient."

"Meaning?" he demanded as ire stirred inside him.

"First you bring me here as if I'm your—what was it you called me? Oh, yes, your companion. Then you provide proof, for those who don't know any better, that something is going on between us."

"I didn't notice you objecting at the time, *cara*. Besides, there is indeed something between us."

"No there's not!"

"Think about it, and I believe you may see it differently."

"I have thought about it, and what I see is just an impulse. We were there and the moment was right."

She had thought of it. It was progress of a sort. "In that case, logic should show you there was no hidden agenda."

"It also shows me," she said with smoldering intensity, "why Italian women often feel like throwing things."

"Be my guest." Andrea picked up his empty bread plate and held it out to her.

She stared at it as if tempted, but then shoved back her chair and got to her feet. "I'm already your guest," she said tightly, "but I won't be for a minute longer than necessary."

A rueful smile tugged at one corner of Andrea's mouth as he put down the bread plate and watched her walk away. Her threat was real, he knew, but he could not regret her flare of anger. She was losing some of her American reserve. For an instant there, she'd seemed as fiery as her red hair, had sounded almost Italian. That change definitely brightened his day.

It was all he could do not to go after her. Yet how could he? She seemed to think he was attracted to her merely because she was available. Following up on it would be like saying he expected her to accept that and fall into his arms anyway.

He didn't, not by a long shot.

What he did expect, he wasn't entirely sure. He only knew he didn't want Dana to go. And he intended to hold her on the island for as long as possible.

The day waned after more interminable hours of avoiding each other. Night drifted in from over the sea. Andrea lingered over a brandy after Dana had gone upstairs, but finally followed after her.

Sleep wouldn't come. He kicked the sheet completely off the bed and threw his pillow across the room. He got up for a drink of water, and then returned to fling himself face down on the mattress. Wrenching over after a few minutes, he sat up and shoved to his feet again. He crouched down to feel around in the dark, sweeping the floor with his spread fingers in search of the discarded pillow.

His hand touched and closed on the down softness just as Guaio let out a screech from down the hall. High-pitched, frantic, it sounded like a cry of distress. Before it died away, Dana shouted out with rage in her voice.

Andrea dropped the pillow and slammed from the bedroom. He raced down the hall and hit Dana's door at a run, throwing it open so hard it bounced off the wall behind it. He skidded to a halt, taking in the flat and empty bed, the open balcony doors where the night breeze off the Mediterranean billowed the curtains into the room.

He saw shadowy figures struggling on the balcony beyond.

Plunging across the room, he launched himself out onto the balcony. His shoulder struck a hard body dressed all in black. The man spun away, but came back at him in a leaping attack. Merciless in his fear for Dana, Andrea bent swiftly, hoisted the assailant high on one his shoulder and tipped him over the balcony railing beside him.

The man yelled as he plummeted to the ground. Andrea didn't bother to look. He whipped around to face Dana.

The second intruder had her around the neck with one arm while clutching Guaio to him with the other. As the man's attention was deflected by the fate of his comrade, Dana grabbed his hand and locked her fingers in his. Whirling out of his hold, she completed the circle and sent the man to his knees with his arm twisted behind his back.

"Drop the cat," she snapped, even as the bones in the man's elbow creaked.

Her would-be assailant grunted and complied. Guaio landed on all fours and streaked into the bedroom, a fleeting gray shadow.

Immediately, the man in black jerked away, breaking Dana's hold. With one wild look in Andrea's direction, he bolted to the railing and flung himself over it. He clung to the wide stone top for an instant then dropped to the ground below. Seconds later, he and the other man could be seen sprinting toward the beach.

Dana stepped to the railing to stare after them. Swinging around, she looked at Andrea. "Do you think—?"

The tremor in her voice before she came to a halt caught at his heart.

"I imagine they have a boat waiting in the cove," he said, moving in beside her. "They will be long gone before anyone can catch them."

"They were after Guaio. He was on the foot of the bed. They came in from the balcony and just grabbed him."

"You should have let them have him." He put out a hand to touch her shoulder, turning her toward him.

"I couldn't," she said. "I just—couldn't."

She came into his arms then, pressing against him from breast to ankles while a fine trembling ran over her. He drew her closer, holding her against him, burying his face in her hair. "I know. You were magnificent, *cara*. You took down the bad guy. Only I think you also took ten years off my life."

"Did I?" The words were not quite even.

"I was afraid they were after you, too."

She gave a convulsive shake of her head. "Just the cat. He—he clawed the face of the one that had him."

"Good for Guaio."

"I was so glad when I saw you."

"Yes."

He let that stark answer stand since he could think of nothing to add to it. The alternative would not bear thinking about, much less comment. He smoothed his hand over her back again and again, taking in her softness along with the fact that she was safe and unharmed.

"You must have been awake to come so quickly," she said after a long moment.

"I was."

"So was I."

Had she been as unable to sleep, and for the same reason? He didn't dare ask.

"I thought for just a second, as I saw the first man, that it was you coming through the balcony door."

His movements ceased as he heard the quiet wonder in her voice. At the same time leftover adrenaline, fervent relief and a warm woman dressed only in a thin nightgown, was having its inevitable effect. His voice was almost too gruff to make sense when he spoke.

"And if it had been?"

She stirred, lifted her head, though her eyes were no more than dark pools in the night. "It would have been all right."

The leap of his heart nearly cracked a rib. He whispered her name, or at least he thought he did; it was hard to hear for the roaring in his ears. Pushing his fingers into her hair, he tilted her head and angled his mouth across hers in hard, frantic need.

She answered it, rising on tiptoe to slide her arms around his neck, humming deep in her throat with a sound like gratified longing. Her lips were smooth and sweet, tasting a little like her toothpaste, as she opened to him. Her skin was fragrant with the intoxicating scent of roses and warm woman. She was firm yet soft against his heated hardness. He could feel the tips of her breasts pressing into his bare chest, sense the wild beat of her heart.

Every atom of his being was at a fever pitch of recognition for her alone. The need to feel the warm satin depths inside her was so strong he was on fire with it, burning everywhere her body touched his.

He was also forgetting the lesson learned before, once more making desperate love to her in full sight of anyone who might care to look. She destroyed his good intentions, obliterated his common sense. With a growl of self-condemnation, he swung her through the open door into the bedroom. There he scooped her up and laid her on the bed.

Guaio hissed and jumped from the mattress to the floor, but Andrea barely noticed. There was only Dana, holding her arms out to him as he settled beside her in the dark.

~ ~ ~

This was what she needed. Dana knew that much with fierce certainty. She recognized it was also what she'd longed for since Guaio interrupted them there on the beach. Her disappointment afterward had been instructive, letting her know how much she had wanted Andrea's touch, the closeness of his body against hers.

Elation and anticipation ballooned inside her. If some small part of it might be purest joy at being safe, unhurt and alive, what did it matter? Life was meant to be embraced.

A temporary fling might not be what she really wanted, but it would be better than going home in a few days without knowing what she'd missed. Any number of wise people had said it was better to regret something you did than something you didn't do. She would take this chance that had come her way then.

Her time with Andrea was limited, a few days set apart here on his private island that was like an enchanted place where maidens could cavort with gods and nothing was quite real. All she could do was take what he offered and make a memory of it to smile over one day while she sat doddering in a nursing home.

She spread her fingers and pressed her palms to the hard muscles of his shoulders, reveling in the intimate contact even as she drew him closer. He snared her waist, shifted his hand lower to draw her against his hard length. She felt the heated nudge of him at the juncture of her thighs and shifted against it, her heart swelling with awe that she could do this to him, with him.

His scent surrounded her, one made of wood and moss and raw desire. She breathed it in, taking it deep just as she wanted to take him. She wanted his mouth on hers again, was parched for that hot incentive. Lifting a hand, she rubbed her palm over the prickly stubble of his evening beard, loving the rasp on her skin, exploring the corner of his mouth with her thumb even as she lifted her mouth to his.

He accepted her invitation, slanting his mouth over hers with unerring accuracy. He took the lead then, invading with a sure, powerful glide of his tongue that made her stomach muscles contract as if it had been a different entry. He took possession, learning her tender surfaces and the sharp edges of her teeth, twining with her tongue in sinuous enticement. She met his raw assault, explored in her turn.

He rolled her to her back, hovering above her as he skimmed his hand down her thigh to reach the hem of her gown. Pushing beneath it, he burrowed upward so the lightweight fabric bunched around his wrist, riding high and higher still. As he reached her breasts, baring them, he brushed their soft mounds with warm lips, nipping a little, soothing with his tongue. With one last lick for each straining peak, he stripped off her gown and sent it flying. Before it had landed, he spread his hand over her abdomen, clasping the slight fullness he found there like a miser holding treasure.

She moaned, moving restlessly on the mattress, wanting his hand centered lower and with more definite intent. He flexed his fingers, holding her in place while he shifted, easing downward on the mattress. An instant later, he lowered his face to the flat of her belly, twirling his tongue into her navel and then blowing carefully on the wetness he'd left behind.

"Andrea," she breathed.

"You are delicious," he said, and went on in a liquid Italian murmur that rippled along her nerve endings, soothing yet inciting. She threaded her fingers through his hair until his skin beaded with goose bumps, then caressed them away as she let her fingers follow the muscles that ridged his back and wrapped around his rib cage.

He brushed his lips along the sensitive skin of her inner thighs, his breath scalding as he trailed to her knees and over their caps, licking the contours. His attentions there made her writhe in protest. "That tickles!"

"It's supposed to," he said with a choke of laughter in his voice, though he soothed away that unbearable irritation. "You were tickling me."

"I didn't mean to," she whispered.

"You can do whatever you like since I intend to match it." His deep, sensually smooth voice turned rough as she shifted her attention to his flat, coin-like nipple, tweaking it. "In fact, I insist on it."

"So whatever I may do, you'll do the same?"

"Or better." The words were a growl.

Her heart throbbed as desire flared inside her like a hot coal in the wind. How could she resist such an erotic threat? Or refuse such freedom?

She had never felt so abandoned or so desired. Exhilaration surged over her in waves. She flattened her hand on his chest, feeling the warm silk of the hair that grew there, locating the hard nub of his nipple again and circling it, wishing she could take it in her mouth. So absorbed was she in what she was doing, it was a moment before she realized he had shifted once more, and now his breath stirred her own fine, silky body hair.

Her breath caught in her throat as he centered his hot, wet attention there. Her stomach muscles clenched and she closed her hands on his shoulders, gripping handfuls of warm skin and muscle. As he slid his hands beneath her hips, raising her to delve deep within her tender folds, her very being seemed to unravel.

Her skin felt on fire. Her blood simmered in her veins. In a delirious maelstrom of the senses, she curled toward him, sliding her hand along his waist to his hip. Encountering the waistband of his silky boxer pajamas, she tugged. As their snap parted, she shoved them aside. Hot, heavy and silken smooth, the length of him seemed to curve toward her as she reached for it.

His breath hissed between his teeth as she touched him

with her tongue. That tried sound made her smile in the dark and redouble her efforts.

Oh, but he did the same and had begun first. Within seconds, she gripped him in hard desperation as her senses imploded with such force she saw flowers of fire behind her eyelids.

Immediately, he eased away from her and turned to hold her close for a breathless instant. She urged him to her with shaking hands. He took her mouth in a fast, deep kiss, and then settled over her, easing between her thighs. With a single twist of his hips, he slid into her tight, hot depths.

Internal pulsations welcomed him, held him as he filled her. Beatitude washed over her in a heated wave, expanding her heart. She lifted against him, taking him deeper. He moved in a slow glide that tested her resilience, yet seemed to seek contact against every possible millimeter of her depths.

She sighed, gasped as he left her room for breathing, keened as he drove deep again. His movements gained power, went deeper still. She grasped his hips, feeling them flex and tighten, holding him seated in her core as she moved against him. He allowed it, aided it for long seconds before withdrawing and then sinking in again.

He was tireless and unhurried, fierce in his concentration, though perspiration gathered on his skin and his muscles leaped and quivered with the constraint he put on his need. Heated, liquid and yielding, she took him, accepted his demanding strokes, returning them with variations of her own. She could feel days, weeks, even months of tension seeping from her, flowing away as it was replaced by the mounting fervor inside her.

Her breath sobbed in her throat. Tears gathered along her eyelids. She curled inward, fastening her mouth on his neck as they jolted together, tasting the salty essence of him on her tongue.

Abruptly, her very being turned on its axis and cleaved to him. She cried out as the orgasm overwhelmed her. His hold tightened. He thrust once more then stiffened with a hard shudder of his body, holding that utmost depth with a fierce contraction of muscles and labored breaths as he bent protectively above her.

Moments passed before he eased from her. With gentle hands, he brushed her hair away from her face, tucking stray strands behind her ear, a gesture so caring it caught at her heart. His breathing had slowed, but he was still damp with perspiration. And so was she, Dana discovered as wind sweeping in at the open door lifted the curtain and swept over her skin.

"You are okay?" he asked, his voice a soft rumble above her ear.

"Fine." It was all she could manage while warm languor still oozed in her veins, though she was sure she had never been more okay in her life.

"You are always fine, no?"

He sounded more Italian than usual. It seemed to happen when he was most moved, or maybe that was only in her mind. She smiled a little at the idea as she answered almost at random. "Most of the time."

"Would you tell me if you were not?"

"It depends." She spread her fingers wide over his chest, captivated by the pulsing of his heartbeat under her palm and the way her every nerve ending and skin cell seemed attuned to his.

"On?"

"I don't know, maybe on what's wrong."

"So I am left to guess."

It hardly seemed to matter since they were unlikely to be together long enough for problems to arise, though she immediately pushed the thought away. "I suppose you could learn to do that in time."

He was quiet, as if absorbing that. Meanwhile, he traced the line of her cheek with a fingertip, brushed her jawbone with his knuckle and then down her neck to her collarbone. He flattened his palm on her chest and then slowly clasped her breast in the prison of his fingers.

"Then I could explain that I did not plan to simply throw you on a bed and make love to you as I did just now. If that was a problem, you would tell me?"

She stared at him in the dark, frustrated at being able to see only shadows where his eyes should be, though she could feel the tingle as he slowly circled the mound of her breast with a fingertip, never quite reaching the top that tightened in hopeful anticipation. "What *did* you plan?"

"There was no plan, only a hope. But if I had intended it, I would have at least have waited for a time when you might be ready, after we had enjoyed fine food, wine and music with, perhaps, a little moonlight."

"You think I need the trappings of romance." It sounded rather lovely, really, now it was too late.

"I think," he said quietly, "that you deserve them."

For some reason, she wanted to cry. "That's very nice of you, but not required."

"I see that, and yet—"

"What?"

"The least I can do is make certain the next time is not quite so hurried."

"That was hurried just now?" she asked with incredulity in her voice. Her heart fluttered inside her ribcage at the idea there would be a next time.

"You did not find it so?"

"Frankly, no."

"Your lovers must have been imbeciles without self-control."

"Lover." She grimaced in the dark as she made that correction.

"Lover? One?"

"He was my fiancé and considered quite the lady's man. Or at least he thought so."

He circled to the bottom of one breast and then across to the other to wind around to its peak. "I believe the phrase is something like 'a legend in his own mind'?"

"You have that right," she said on a low chuckle.

"And afterward?"

"He wanted to get married right away. I—didn't, as I told you before."

"A lifetime of sex too soon over did not appeal."

"Then or later." It hadn't been entirely her fiancé's fault, she thought. He had tried, but somehow foreplay to him was merely a job he had to do to get her ready. In his frustration, he sometimes lost it. Sex became something neither of them could win, since the harder she tried to hurry her arousal, the more difficult it became to respond at all. Too often she simply let him have what he wanted while she felt next to nothing.

"We must see what we can do to erase that experience."

He bent his head and took her nipple into the heat of his mouth, drawing on it with gentle suction, flicking it with his tongue before drawing on it again. Molten desire stirred inside her like the slow building of a volcano, though doubt based on experience threatened to cap it.

"You don't mean now?" she asked as she touched the plane of his face, fascinated by the sensation as she felt the working of his jaw.

He pressed against her, nudging her with the hot shaft that lay between them while heat rose off him in waves.

Her breath caught in her throat. "You do mean now!"

"We are together in this bed, you and I," he said against the moist, tight tip of her breast, "and the night has just begun."

~ ~ ~

He couldn't get enough of her. She was so natural in her responses, so generous—so very polite, just as her T-shirt had promised. There was no coquetry in her reactions, no overt awareness of their roles as male and female, and yet she was more deeply, naturally sensual than any woman he'd ever known.

She was guarded at times, but he suspected it was from self-protection. The way she shied away from speaking of what she wanted or needed from him caught at his heart. To discover that she would answer if pushed far enough was his secret pleasure, one he intended to hold close until she realized it on her own. She would, Andrea thought, and soon. She was as intelligent in bed as she was elsewhere.

She slept now, curled against his side with her knee across his thigh. The vulnerability of that position was a torturous enticement, but he resisted the urge to wake her with an intimate caress. Later, it might be impossible to resist, but he was replete for now. At least he was in body, if not in mind.

She drove him to frenzied, brainless need, truly she did. He'd been so enthralled with her during the past hour that he had nearly forgotten the men who had dared invade the villa. They were long gone, he was sure, but he could have at least closed and locked the door.

Protection had also escaped his mind. The dangerous excitement beforehand had some bearing, also being in Dana's bedroom instead of his own where he had access to condoms, but these things could not excuse him entirely.

He was not so self-centered as to expect his partner to arrange such matters. This was his responsibility and he had failed. It was something he must discuss with Dana when morning came.

Her slow, even breathing tickled the hair on his chest,

but he endured it, just as he endured the numbness of his arm where her head rested upon it. The trust in the way she had turned to him, sighed and slept breached some place inside that had never been touched. He was content to the point of amazement to simply lie there and hold her. Some things were worth any discomfort.

A part of it was that he had no idea how long it would last. She gave no sign of being impressed by what he had or how he lived. He was fervently glad of that, but it also gave him no possible hold upon her.

Moving with slow care, he picked up a strand of her hair and rubbed it between his fingers. Drawing it out to its full length, then, he draped it over his chest, letting it fall to lie on his abdomen. It was a yearning realized. Or another one, really, as making love to her had been the greatest of his dreams.

It was one he still held, as he was far from sated with tasting her freckles and other pale places untouched by any sun, might never be entirely satisfied.

Smiling wryly in the dark at his satyr's urges, he closed his eyes.

Sleep still eluded him. As his libido quieted, his mind replayed the sight of Dana struggling with the two assailants in black. He felt again the savage fear that had sent him unarmed onto the balcony.

They had been after Guaio, and nearly had him. That Dana had risked so much, possibly even her life, to save a cat was the stuff of nightmares.

Something would have to be done.

Dana was right; he needed to intervene in this business between Bella and Rico. It had gone too far, much too far.

He should do it now, while rage burned hot inside him. If Rico was behind the business he deserved a few hard words about his methods, as Dana had suggested. That was not all he would hear, either. There were ways to make certain he stopped what he was doing or paid the price.

Tomorrow would be soon enough. Tomorrow, when he was cooler and would say nothing that Bella might wish unsaid. Tomorrow, when he was no longer a pillow for the woman in his arms. Tomorrow, when he would have to let her go. He closed his eyes, squeezing them tight.

"Andrea! Andrea, wake up!"

He came upright with his heart throbbing in his chest. The alarm in Dana's voice triggered his own, along with a slicing edge of terror for her.

She was not in the bed beside him. He heaved over, shoving to one elbow, and then exhaled in sudden sharp relief as he saw her silhouetted against the light coming through the open doorway.

He ran a hasty gaze over her, searching for injuries. He saw none but did notice the sexy curves of her naked bottom as she stood with her back to him, along with the intriguing inked outline of her girl-on-a-dolphin tattoo that covered the base of her spine.

"What is it? What happened?" he demanded in annoyed despair over the unmistakable stirring below his waist.

"Look!"

He was looking, though he was trying to direct his

attention elsewhere. It was fully five seconds before he noticed the dust that boiled around the curtain in a pale yellow cloud, heard its telltale whisper and patter against the floor and exterior villa walls, or saw the growing darkness outside where there should have been the brightness of morning sun.

"Close the shutters," he said, whipping back the covers as he powered to his feet. "Then shut the door. Do it now, at once."

She did as he said, batting aside the curtain that swayed in the rising wind, stepping out to drag the shutters together. He was beside her, then, holding them while she slammed the bolts into place. He swung the glass-paned door closed and twisted the lock.

The double barrier closed the wind outside. In the sudden quiet, he looked down at Dana, taking in her wide eyes. "Don't look like that, it's all right."

"What was that? I mean, what is it?"

"The *Scirocco*," he said, "or Sirocco, as you would say in English. It comes now and then in August."

"I thought that was just wind."

He tipped his head in assent. "Hot wind out of Africa, though sometimes it brings dust from the Sahara."

"You mean we are standing in dust from the Sahara desert?"

They were indeed. It had spread across the floor in a thin sheet marked by windblown waves. It also lay in small piles against their feet. And that wasn't the only place it had landed.

"The very same," he answered, and reached to skim the back of his finger down the rounded slope of her breast so sand drifted from it like gold dust, sifting down into the captivating curls that proved she was a natural redhead. "It looks as if it was doing its best to bury you."

"And you," she said, reaching to brush away the coating on the tops of his shoulders, glancing pointedly at the dusting that lay atop his semi-erection.

"It's also burying my bedroom," he said in sudden realization. "I must close the door there."

He turned away with reluctance, though he caught her hand to pull her along with him. Together, they slammed shutters and doors closed to bar the sand from that room as well. When it was done, he turned to her once more.

"As sad as it might be to wash this African dirt down the drain after it has come so far, I believe we are in need of a shower."

Her grimace as she wiped dust from her arms was agreement enough.

"I could be all gallant and say ladies first, but—" He stopped, lifted a brow.

Her movements slowed. Daring gleamed in the rich brown of her eyes, while pale rose color filtered through the dust on her face. She swallowed with a quick movement in the line of her throat, and then reached to take his hand again. Turning toward his en suite bath, she glanced at him over her shoulder.

"The lady has a better idea."

It was far better, that joint shower, but not nearly as fast as two separate ones might have been.

He rubbed shampoo through her hair and kissed her while her eyes were screwed too tightly closed to see what he was about. She soaped the hair on his chest and pushed her fingers through it until he thought he would explode.

Shower gel made a lovely, slick surface for exploration of her curves and hollows, though she couldn't hold still for laughing at his tickling progress. She half drowned him, making him kneel while she rinsed the shampoo from his hair.

That was her mistake, however, for the position gave him an unfair advantage that he seized without mercy.

By the time the water finally ran cool, he had her exactly where he'd wanted her from the moment he'd seen the sand coating the rounded hills of her breasts, had her with her back against the shower's warm tile and her legs around his waist. The splashing of the water around them, joining the sounds of wet flesh against wet flesh and half-strangled moans, sent him spinning into the a possessive fury. He wanted to mark this woman as his for all time, to make it impossible for her ever to make love again without thinking of him.

He needed her to come undone in his arms in a way unlike any other, one that could never be repeated. It was crazy and he knew it, but that did not prevent him from plunging into her until he thought his heart would burst.

When he had what he wanted, when she shuddered and cried out as he held her, he rested his forehead against hers and leaned into her because it was the only way he could keep from collapsing to the shower floor. And he cursed himself for ten kinds of fool because, though he had used protection this time, being in his own bathroom with condoms mere feet away, he wished devoutly it had not been necessary.

EIGHT

*D*ana returned to her own room well before Luisa, Tommaso and the others were due to arrive for the day. Andrea left out at the same time, saying something about checking the helicopter to be certain its tie-downs were holding and there was no damage from the ongoing storm. He'd removed her shoulder bandage first, however, leaving the scratches uncovered as they were well enough for it. He kissed them again to make them better, however, and then kissed her with breathtaking thoroughness, making her better as well.

As she brushed tangles from her hair and smoothed cream on the beard burns she'd found here and there, she glanced at her reflection in the bathroom mirror. She looked no different, yet is seemed she moved in a sensual haze. Her body and mind were so sensitized to Andrea that a mere look or brush of his hand was enough to send her into trembling readiness. She had lost count of the times they made love in the night. As for what had happened in his shower—

No, she wouldn't think about that, couldn't without flushing from head to toe. She'd never dreamed it could be that way between lovers, teasing and laughing one moment, wild with driving desire the next.

A smile of purest feminine pleasure curved her mouth as she thought of his concern afterward, his fear that he'd been too rough or not careful enough. She was made of stronger stuff than that. She was indeed, even if she was aware of soreness in muscles she hadn't known she had and tenderness where she'd never felt it before.

She felt a lot of things she'd not known until now. It stunned her to realize how many, and how close she had come to never experiencing them.

No matter what happened, she would always have the night before to remember.

Guaio, watching her from where he lay in a regal sprawl on the foot of the bed, gave a plaintive meow. Dana chuckled as she moved toward the huge old *armadio* that served as a closet for the clothing Andrea had provided.

"I know, and I'm sorry," she said over her shoulder. "It was most unkind to dislodge you last night after your scare."

The cat mewed again while he flicked his tail up and down with every sign of irritated agreement.

"Yes, and unfair as well. I don't blame you at all for finding somewhere else to spend the night. It can't have been too restful for you, with everything that was going on."

She took down a simple and lightweight shift in sand-colored linen as something that should be cool in spite of the heat, tossing it across the bed next to the cat.

Meow...

"Enduring a sand storm with no one about must have been disturbing, I agree. I am here now, though, and so is Andrea." She smiled at the truth of that as she slipped into a flesh-colored bra and matching panties, then reached for the shift to pull it on over her head.

Meow...

"Well, I don't know how long this state of affairs will last," she told the cat with airy unconcern. "No, nor what will happen later. But I do suggest you find other accommodation for tonight, just in case I have company in my bed again."

"An excellent suggestion."

Dana gasped at that low-voiced, drawling comment, but then laughed. Thrusting her head and arms into place in the shift, she sent Andrea a look of mock severity. "I didn't know you were there. You startled me."

He leaned on the doorframe, his heated green gaze following her movements as she shimmied into the shift that was so loosely woven it came close to being transparent. "I would show you how likely you are to have me in your bed instead of Guaio, except breakfast is ready."

"Really? Already?"

"Rolls, fruit and coffee only, but we must keep up our strength."

She flushed, she couldn't help it. It wasn't from

embarrassment, however, but at the promise in his eyes that told her why they must be strong. Also at her wayward imagination that pictured him removing her linen dress and underwear with sure movements of his strong, beautiful hands. Yes, and her own slow removal of the white linen shirt and pants he wore. His skin would be firm, warm and incredibly enticing in its muscular firmness beneath the soft fabric. She would—

Yes, she would. Later.

Anticipation was a potent aphrodisiac.

"Breakfast it is," she said with a warm glance from under her lashes. "Lead me to it."

The Sirocco continued through the morning, howling around the eaves of the villa and sifting fine dust in around doors and windows in spite of the shutters that protected them. The sun sometimes appeared as the winds died away, but vanished again on their return. In between, the world was a featureless gray-brown vista of blowing sand. It whispered and sang, smelling of dirt and camel dung and the bones of ancient Bedouins.

Or maybe the latter two were only her odd fancy brought on by the close confinement; Dana could not be absolutely certain.

Andrea called Luisa and the others, telling them to stay put in their homes for the duration as there would be much to do when the storm blew itself out. Dana heard him on the phone in his office again a short time later, his voice quietly commanding and not particularly cordial. Yet when he appeared again he was as relaxed as ever.

"Did anyone else on the island see the men last night?" she asked, searching his face for some clue as to what was on his mind.

"A fisherman out checking on his boat saw them. He didn't report it until this morning as they were leaving at the time, and he was weather-wise enough to know sirocco wind was gaining strength, so going out after them would be hazardous."

"But they will keep watch on the cove now."

"Especially at night." He hesitated. "I also spoke to Rico."

"And?" she asked as he failed to elaborate.

Andrea shoved his hands into his pockets, scowling at the stone floor with its scattering of dust. "He claims to know nothing about any break-in."

"You don't believe him?"

"It doesn't make sense. There is no one else. Unless—"

She watched him, loving the concentration in his face, loving the way he faced problems, by applying action and logic with a leavening of intuition.

Loving him, she realized with the sudden race of blood in her veins.

How had that happened when they had spent such a short time together? Was it brought on by their semi-isolation? Or might it stem from the heightened emotions caused by the danger they had been through?

One thing she knew well; it was not some ridiculous version of Stockholm syndrome. People tossed that phrase around so casually these days, but most had no idea what it meant. She'd studied the phenomenon at the police academy, and this was entirely different. She felt no need whatever to court Andrea's good will or align her identity with his to keep him from harming her, had never been completely in his power. She had not been confined, nor had she been prevented from notifying friends and family of her safety. She had been brought to the island against her will, true, but it had been for her protection.

No, what she felt was something more, something so vital it was as if she had been waiting all her life for Andrea to happen to her. If she believed in destiny, she would say that she had found hers. And even if it was only for this small space of days, she meant to meet it head-on.

The villa grew overwarm and airless without the sea breeze blowing through to temper the August heat. Though there was an air conditioning system available, the prospect of sand being pulled into its machinery made using it out of the question. Andrea shed his shirt soon enough. Dana was fairly cool in her loose dress, though she pulled her hair up into a ponytail. They both alternated between staring out the one or two small windows that had no shutters, sipping cold drinks that varied from water and juice to limoncello, and fanning themselves with whatever was handy.

Toward noon, Andrea disappeared in the direction of the kitchen. Guaio leaped down and trotted after him, deserting Dana where she sat trying to read. At first, she was glad to have the cat's furry heat removed from where he had been lying along her thigh. When neither man nor beast returned, however, she laid her book aside and went in search of them.

The scent of garlic and onions simmering in olive oil greeted her in the kitchen. She stood an instant in the doorway, surveying what was surely a modernized version of an old island cooking space. To the beamed ceiling, stone floors and high windows with thick-paned glass had been added stainless steel appliances and a triple stainless sink. The sturdy wood cabinets were white trimmed in gray and topped by gray granite, while some of their doors had new-looking glass fronts. A trio of long rubber mats cushioned the hard stone in front of the range, sink and stainless prep table that centered the room.

Andrea looked up, smiling a welcome from where he diced tomatoes at the prep table. Behind him, a large stainless steel pot sat on the restaurant style range. Steam rose from it, and the sauté pan next to it sizzled with its gently frying vegetables. Guaio lay under the table, as if patiently waiting.

"Something smells delicious," she said as she strolled to the table.

"Spaghetti." He shrugged. "Nothing particularly impressive."

"It impresses me." That was the truth, but not the whole of it. She was also impressed by the precision and economy of motion he brought to the task. Not to mention the concentration on his face and the way the muscles in his arms glided under the skin as they did his bidding.

Any man engaged in cooking for a woman was seriously sexy, but he was a stellar example.

She reached to filch a cube of tomato from the cutting board in front of him and pop it into her mouth. Humming her appreciation as she chewed, she put out her hand for another.

"Stop that," he said, tapping her fingers with the flat of the wicked-looking chef's knife in his hand.

"You have plenty." In fact, he had three more Roma tomatoes lined up that he hadn't begun to dice.

There was heat in the look he slanted at her. "That's not what I meant. It's that sound you make when you are—pleased."

"Oh."

She hadn't been trying to turn him on. She thought of protesting, but it seemed more interesting to see what it might take to actually accomplish that. After all, the only thing he had to do was stand there without a shirt, exposing his washboard abs as if they were nothing special. It didn't seem quite fair.

Turning so her back was to the prep table, she allowed her gaze to travel over his shoulders and down his chest to the narrow line of hair that bisected his six-pack before disappearing under the drawstring waist of his linen pants. Almost unconsciously, she licked her bottom lip.

He stared at her mouth as he chopped, his gaze lingering. Until he suddenly exclaimed in Italian with the sound of a curse and dropped the knife.

"Did you cut yourself?"

Remorse added urgency to her voice. She pushed away from the table and followed him as he swung quickly to the sink and turned on the water, letting it run over his fingers.

"Just a nick."

"Let me see."

He was right. It was only a small slice on the tip of his index finger. She circled his waist with her arms, laying her head on his shoulder. "I'm sorry. I shouldn't have been teasing you while you had a dangerous weapon in your hand."

"Is that what you were doing?" he asked, craning his neck to give her a look from under his lashes.

"Sort of." She smiled against his warm skin.

"That's what I thought."

The muscles of his back under her cheek moved as he reached to turn off the water and then pick up a towel to dry his hands.

"I could kiss it and make it better," she murmured. "I have it on good authority that works."

"*Dio, cara,* no!" he said in rough rejection.

Her hold loosened and she raised her head while hurt tightened her voice. "Unless you'd rather I didn't."

He leaned away from her to switch off the blue flames that heated the water for the spaghetti, also those under his sauté pan.

"It isn't that," he said in low certainty as he turned back to enclose her in his arms. "It's only I can think of better uses for your kisses."

He mated his mouth to hers with the hunger of a man near starvation. Their tongues tangled, meshed, and played catch-as-catch-can. And all the while, he was sliding the fabric-covered elastic from her hair, molding her breasts and their aching nipples to fit his palms.

She untied the drawstring of his linen pants before dipping into them for what she sought. He groaned as she found him, but was already skimming her dress off over her head and dropping it on the floor. Her panties and bra quickly followed before he cupped her cool and rounded hips, pulling her into the cradle of his own as he leaned against the cabinet behind him.

Their breathing was fast and uneven, an obbligato of sighs and whispers, gasps and humming moans. He found the hollow behind her ear, explored it, drew her earlobe into his mouth, gold hoop earring and all, and laved it with his tongue until she writhed against his strutted heat.

She kissed his chest, bent her head to take his tightly budded nipple into her mouth while he threaded his fingers into her hair and told her things she understood only on a primal level and because she felt them in her heart.

Tugging at his pants, she shoved them down to his ankles, and would have followed them to kneel before him if he had not held her upright. Pushing away from the cabinet, he bent to retrieve a condom from his pants. He stepped from them then kicked the long, spongy rubber floor mat more into the walkway. He took her down to it with him, turning to his back so she stretched full length upon his hard form.

What other invitation did she need? She straddled him, her knees on the soft mat and calves aligned with his as she licked and suckled and took him deep, enjoying the sounds he made, the breath hissing between his teeth, his strained sighs and soft groans. He threaded his fingers through her hair but did not compel or direct in anyway, seemed content to allow whatever she pleased, as she pleased.

Until he had enough.

He lifted her higher with hard hands before driving into her slick depths. She gasped at the sudden filling, rose a little and settled upon him more firmly. Bracing her hands on his shoulders, holding tight, she closed her eyes, savoring the sensation that was like being locked to him.

She lifted her lashes then and swung her hair behind her back. Gazing down into the dark green depths of his eyes, she memorized the moment, tucking it away so it would be safe forever. And then she began to move.

"*Per Dio*," he whispered as he smoothed his hands along her firm thighs that gripped him, grasped her hips to steady her, "I have dreamed of this since the moment I first saw the girl-on-a-dolphin on your back."

~ ~ ~

Dana did not answer him, but Andrea hardly expected it. She was nearing extremis, he thought, that moment when surging pleasure wiped away all thought. He could feel its pulsating approach, just as he could feel the hot, beating core of her. Clinging to control by the smallest of margins, he waited, not out of male pride but from the need to know the moment when she was truly his if only for that brief interval. It helped that he could distract himself by flashing glances at her reflection in the glass of the cabinet doors where he could see not only her wild ride but the tattoo that enthralled him. To see and feel at the same time was a special privilege.

The moment came with a single warning contraction. She rode it to the end, her gaze holding his with an expression of ecstasy so intense and unyielding it seemed near pain. And when she began to fail, he rolled with her until her back was to the resilient surface of the mat.

He finished it then, lifting her knees for the greatest penetration, supporting himself on his elbows while he carried them both higher than they had reached before, until his brain was on fire, his breath turned to steam in his lungs, and he felt the contractions begin again, taking him in, holding him with her deep intimate caress that he craved beyond life itself.

In that moment, he saw tears shimmering in her eyes as she lay under him, so incredibly beautiful, so incredibly taken in love, and he knew his own face had that same look of agonized joy as hers just minutes before.

Sometime later, he lowered her legs until she lay full length, enjoying the smoothness of her body against his heated skin for an instant. He eased to his side then but took her with him, facing him, reluctant to lose the connection of their bodies. She held him to her with her spread fingers on his hip, as if she was also loath to be apart. And feeling that possessive clasp, his heart swelled with the rightness of it.

He kissed the top of her head, inhaled the delicate scent of her hair. Feeling tension in the strands that lay under her, he tugged gently until they were free and then pushed them back, combing them free of tangles with his fingers. Words crowded his mind, hovered on his tongue, but they were all in Italian. She wouldn't understand, and he needed to be certain that she did. His English seemed to have fled, and he breathed deep to send oxygen to his brain so translation might return.

"*Cara mia*," he said finally, "do you know the words *Ti amo*?"

She shifted a little, tilting her head back to look at him. "Should I?"

"I have not said them before, if that is what you mean," he answered with a fleeting smile. "However, I say them now, and—"

He halted as a noise like a slamming door came from the front of the villa. It was followed at once by a trilling call.

"Andrea! Where are you?"

Bella.

The curse he muttered was ancient, idiomatic and biting. It was also no more than a whisper as any sound would instantly bring his sister toward the kitchen.

Disengaging in haste, he sat up, gathered Dana's clothing and thrust the bundle into her hands. "My sister. Into the laundry while I stall her," he said as he surged to his feet, pulling her with him.

She grasped the point before the words were out of his mouth. While shaking out his pants and hopping on one foot to put them on, he had the pleasure of seeing her swift exit in the direction he indicated, with the bright light that came now through the kitchen window shining on the red mane of her hair and glazing the skin of her back, bottom and legs with the sheen of fine pearls.

He swore again, though this time with reverence and regret.

"Andrea?"

This call was nearer. Bella was coming toward the kitchen, probably attracted by the smell of cooking.

He scooped up his boxers left lying on the rubber mat in his haste. Seeing no place to hide them, he tossed them into the trash can that sat in a pull-out bin below the prep table surface. Raking one hand through his hair for at least some kind of order, he turned the fire back on under his sauté pan with the other. Then he reached for the lever of the kitchen faucet, hoping Bella would take the splash of running water as a reason why he hadn't heard her.

"What are you doing, Andrea? The sirocco is done. Why is the place still shut up like a tomb?"

He glanced over his shoulder in feigned surprise while scrubbing his hands under the water. "*Ciao*, Bella, where did you come from?"

His sister swept into the kitchen and immediately deposited her Hermés handbag and an Aventi knitting bag on the end of a cabinet. She looked as if she had stepped from the cover of a fashion magazine, her dark hair precisely coiffed, her nails perfectly manicured with an unlikely chocolate-colored polish, her dress the latest fashion worn with outré shoes and beaded jewelry constructed from knitted gold wire.

Andrea recognized, with no great surprise, that he had

developed a distinct preference for natural, unadorned beauty.

"Naples, of course," she answered, clicking toward him on her ridiculous four-inch heels and leaning to greet him with a kiss on either cheek. "I set out the instant I got off the phone with my miserable pig of a husband. What is this you were telling him about last night? I never heard such a story!"

He shut off the water, reached for a hand towel to dry his hands. "Every word of it was the truth."

"I can't believe it, truly I cannot. Rico is a great fool who thinks he can tell me what I must do every waking moment, but he is not a criminal."

"No?" He watched her with care as he waited for an answer.

"I swear it." Turning from him, she reached for a spatula and stirred the onions and garlic that had begun to sizzle again in the sauté pan. "What's this you are making? Oh, I see. Lovely. But you know the water for your pasta will heat sooner if you actually turn on the fire under it?"

"You will join us, of course. I'll chop more tomato." His voice was laconic as he watched her switch on the burner and then taste the water for saltiness. His sister was one of those women who felt the kitchen was their domain, one where men should never venture without their instruction.

"Naturally," she said, reaching for the salt box. "But where is the woman you have here with you. I assume this is who you mean when you speak in the plural?"

"I'm here," Dana said, strolling out of the laundry with

Guaio in her arms. "Just look at this stuffed feline. I found him serving himself lunch out of the cat food bag."

"Petrarca!"

Bella abandoned the salt box and hurried forward to take her cat from Dana. "There you are, my precious. What a relief to see you. Your mama has been so very worried. She would murder Rico with her bare hands if he harmed a single hair on your beautiful body."

Andrea was relieved to see humor brightened Dana's eyes instead of insult at being ignored for a cat. He performed the introduction with a wave of his knife, and then diced tomatoes while on guard against the possibility that Bella might show her claws.

He need not have worried.

"You are the American who saved my Petrarca?" She took the hand Dana held out to her, but drew her close for the usual double kisses of greeting. "What happiness to meet you. I so feared I would not, that you might have gone before I arrived. But I see Andrea is looking after you. He is all obligation, my brother, so concerned for everyone who comes into his orbit. I hope you have enjoyed your stay here on the island?"

The look Dana sent him was a trifle arch, yet still amused. She did not appear to hold it against him that he omitted telling Bella he had abducted her. "Oh, yes," she said. "Immensely."

Andrea clenched his teeth, swearing silently as he felt himself respond to the undertone of sensual content in that last word. Immensely, indeed!

"But this terrible sirocco! You cannot have enjoyed that," Bella went on, heedless of everything except her own concerns. "How I hate this wind! And the sand, faugh! We did not have sand in Naples, and so I set out not knowing how it would be. I could not hire a helicopter, for none would take off, so came on by boat. Thank God it was over by the time we landed, so Tommaso could come for me in the golf cart when I called. But now I see sand is everywhere in the house. I sent Tommaso to tell Luisa she must attend to the cleaning."

"She may begin after lunch." Andrea let her know by the tone of his voice that he would tolerate no more interference.

"*Certo*, my dear brother. I meant after we have eaten your so delicious pasta."

Bella rattled on at once, inquiring into every detail of the accident on the coast road, the appearance of the men in the boat, and the attempt to carry off Guaio. She shuddered and exclaimed over Dana's courage in fighting off the attackers until Andrea's arrival, and combed her pet's hair with her long, brown nails all the while.

Guaio mewed plaintively and followed Dana with his blue eyes. It was clear he would rather be in her arms, a feeling Andrea well understood. Still he hoped Guaio remained with his mistress for the sake of peace.

Dana moved around the prep table, coming to a halt on the opposite side from Bella. Andrea gave her a slanting glance, thinking she looked cool and put-together, even if her linen shift was more than a bit wrinkled. Her hair was even back in its pony tail.

She was beautiful and altogether desirable, but he much preferred her naked.

She flushed a little under his gaze, and busied herself sweeping up the peelings from the onions, garlic and tomatoes. Tipping out the trash bin, she started to rake everything inside.

She glanced down, but then looked up again with wide eyes. Her gaze centered on his waist where his tan line could plainly be seen since he'd had no time to tie the drawstring of his linen pants as well as usual.

Without doubt, she had seen his boxers in the trash.

The pink tip of her tongue came out to moisten her lips while her eyes turned dark. The movements of his knife ceased.

"Andrea? Are you going deaf? I asked if you have bread to go with the spaghetti." Bella tapped the toe of her expensive shoe on the stone floor, but her bright gaze darted from him to Dana and back again.

He gave his sister a caustic look. His mind was not on bread. He wished her a hundred miles away while he wondered if the stainless top of the prep table was too chilly for the fantasy that had slammed into his brain.

"Never mind, I will look for it," Bella said while a slow smile tilted her mouth. "Yes, and for a nice Chianti, as well. What is pasta without bread and wine?"

Andrea heard the departing click of his sister's heels. He returned to his cooking, scooping diced chunks of tomato onto his chef's knife and tossing them into the sauté pan.

He sniffed the aroma then added more herbs, not because he thought they were needed but because it was his sauce, his kitchen, his meal for Dana.

When he turned from the range, she was watching him. Hunger lingered in her clear brown eyes, but he did not think for a moment it was for his spaghetti. He breathed deep, regretting the interruption of their idyll yet again. And he willed his too-obvious appetite for her to subside, all the while knowing it was unlikely.

They ate on the terrace, as the wind had died away, just as Bella had said, and the sun appeared so bright it might have been sand-blasted to a high polish. It was a surprisingly relaxed meal with Bella on her best behavior. She even brought her knitting project to the table, a fine lace shawl in gray wool spun with metallic silver to which she added stitches whenever she put down her fork.

The only strained moment occurred when Guaio insisted on sitting at Dana's feet to be fed with tidbits from her plate. Though the cat had never shown the slightest urge for pasta before, he ate lengths of spaghetti from her hand as if they were basted with catnip.

"You need not feel slighted, Bella," Andrea said. "Guaio prefers Dana to me as well." He understood the cat only too well since he would also have enjoyed being fed by Dana.

"I wish you will not call him that," his sister said with a pettish frown. "His name is Petrarca."

"Yes, of course," he murmured, "though I'm not sure he will answer to it now." He reached to scratch behind a brown ear with one finger. "Will you, boy?"

After lunch, Luisa, Tommaso and a pair of extra women arrived from the village. They took over cleaning the kitchen, as well as clearing the sand from the villa. Andrea, Bella and Dana lingered on the terrace, well out of their way. Lemon sherbet soon appeared, along with coffee and mineral water. They sat back in their chairs, enjoying the light fare, the breeze, clear sand-free air and each other. The three of them were still at the table under the pergola when they heard the dull roar and whopping beat of an approaching helicopter.

Andrea, mindful of the plane that had buzzed the house before, rose and walked from the shade, narrowing his eyes to track the aircraft. Its colors marked it as belonging to a lease fleet, and it made for the helipad as if directed by someone who knew the island's topography.

The chopper settled in a maneuver that signaled an experienced pilot at the controls. The blades slowed. The side door eased open. A dark-haired man, square-built and solid in tobacco brown pants and matching sports shirt, stepped out.

"*Che Diavolo!*" Bella exclaimed in disgust, setting her knitting on the table and rising to her feet. "What is he doing here?"

The question was almost lost as the helicopter revved up and took off again the instant its passenger was clear. Andrea glanced at Dana met his gaze with a question in her eyes.

"Not the devil, but Rico," he explained, his voice laconic. "You are about to meet my sister's husband."

"How dare you show your face here?" Bella shouted before the man was halfway across the lawn. "I should call the police! You deserve to be in prison for what you have done. I can't believe you have so little concern for me and my family that you would bring hired guns into this business between us. It is a madness greater than I would ever have dreamed, even of you!"

"*Ciao*, Bella," her husband said, his voice dry yet strained as he mounted to the terrace from the side steps.

"Don't come near me," she cried, retreating behind a chair.

"Bella, my love—"

"Do not '*Bella, my love*' me, you cretin." She turned toward Andrea. "Tell him to leave. Make him go away."

"Well, Rico?" Andrea moved to block his brother-in-law's advance.

"I had to come, had to see Bella and you and the American lady." Rico glanced beyond him to where Dana had remained in her seat. Disturbed by the arrival of the helicopter, perhaps, Guaio had leaped into her lap and was reclining there, kneading her knee. "This is she?"

"As you say." The introduction Andrea made was brief and barely civil.

"*Signorina*," his brother-in-law began before switching to heavily accented English, "I must thank you with all my heart for preventing the capture of my wife's beloved pet, and this not once but twice. If the men sent by my father had succeeded, I would be without hope. You have done me a service beyond price."

"Not at all," Dana said evenly. "But are you saying it wasn't you who tried to harm Guaio?"

"Never would I do such a thing. I could not, though I have no great fondness for him."

"You dare to claim it was your papa, instead." Bella said with disdain.

Rico spread his hands, reverting to Italian as he answered. "It pains me to admit it, but—"

"He is a despicable old Mafioso with ideas about women that belong in the Victorian Age. But you cannot put your dirty work off on him!"

"It was not mine, I tell you. Papa—Papa is desperate for the return of the collar your precious Petrarca wears."

"What! This collar you gave him?" Bella glanced at the gem-studded collar the cat wore, as did they all.

"It's about Guaio's collar," Andrea said in a quiet aside as she turned to him with raised brows. "It belonged to his father."

Rico grimaced as he watched his wife. "I should never have taken it, would not have had I guessed its value. It seemed only a pretty bauble, one I had seen often on my papa's desk as I was growing up. I never thought—had no idea what it meant to him."

"But to go so far for such a paltry reason. It's unbelievable."

"There is nothing paltry about something set with twenty blue diamonds."

"B-Blue—" Bella stuttered to a halt, obviously at a loss for words.

"Diamonds," Andrea said to Dana with a gesture toward the collar. "Blue diamonds."

"This? You're sure?" She touched the gems inset in the leather with careful fingertips.

"So Rico says."

Rico lifted his shoulders and let them fall as he stared from Bella to Dana and then to Andrea. "I see I must tell you everything. If I had come to you in the beginning, Andrea, things might have been different."

"Yes, yes, just get on with it," Bella interrupted with an impatient gesture.

"As you will." Rico inclined his head. "It seems that some decades ago, in the 1950s, there was a jewel thief who targeted the wealthy English and Americans that wintered in Positano and Amalfi," Rico began. "He terrorized those who lived in the big houses along the coast, for he came and went as they slept, eluded all guards, took only the best and rarest of gems. He was never heard, never seen—except for one time, and that by an elderly lady who said she only saw his shadow. The called him the Ghost of Amalfi."

Andrea moved to stand beside Dana as he translated. This looked to be an involved tale.

"A cat burglar," she said on a low laugh as she glanced up at him.

"You have it exactly right, *Signorina*," Rico said with a small bow in her direction, "which is why—but I get ahead of myself."

"*Per favore*, Rico!" Bella exclaimed.

"*Si, si*, my love," he said, falling back into Italian. "The fame of this cat burglar grew ever greater for six long years. Then one winter the thefts stopped. The Ghost of Amalfi was not heard from again. By no coincidence, this was the year my grandfather, my papa's father, met and married my grandmother, a lady as devout as she was beautiful."

"Your grandfather was the burglar."

"A career he gave up without regret, though he still had contacts, friends, relatives who had known him in those days, and who are also known to my papa."

"Mafioso, just as I have always said!"

"Perhaps at one time, but no more," Rico allowed with a pained expression. "But my grandfather kept for himself one small memento of those nights when he ghosted in and out of the bedrooms of the wealthy, a piece of tremendous value that was his private joke for his days as a cat burglar. It was as unusual as it was useless, so much so it might be used even now to connect him to those crimes of long ago."

"My Petrarca's collar."

"Of a certainty, and a family treasure that he passed on to his son, my papa, when he died."

"I begin to see," Andrea said slowly.

"You would, of course, as you understand family honor. But I had never heard this tale, never knew about my grandfather's past. When the collar came up missing, my papa was beside himself. I had to confess what I had done with this valuable piece that I thought was set with rhinestones, CZs, glass, anything but diamonds. I might have asked Bella to return it, but we were separated and she would not speak to me. My papa was desperate to retrieve the collar before it was recognized, and so—"

"So he sent men to kill him to get it?" Bella exclaimed. "Horrible!"

"As you say. But you must understand he gave no order that the cat was to die. The men he entrusted with the task of bringing back the collar misunderstood."

"You are quite sure?"

Rico looked uncomfortable. "Papa may have suggested it would be a good thing if the cat disappeared for a while. He knows poor Pertarca has been a bone of contention between us."

"What did he think? That we would be reconciled in our grief?"

"Or you would realize I am a better husband when not wheezing from an allergy to cat hair."

"Now you are suddenly allergic."

"Not suddenly, no. I have been allergic all this time, my love. But how could I complain when Petrarca meant so much to you?"

Bella set one hand on her hip while waving the other in the air. "You really expect me to believe this nonsense that is coming out of your mouth?"

Andrea thought he might accept it if only because Rico lacked the imagination to come up with such a story on his own. More than that, he had the desperate look of a man fighting for his happiness. That his sister might relent seemed possible as well, if only because she had ceased to shout at him.

Noticing the inquiring look Dana turned in his direction,

he realized he had failed to translate the last few rapid-fire exchanges. He would explain the details to her as soon as possible. For now, it seemed best that he referee.

To Rico, he said, "You told your father all attempts to take Guaio must cease?"

"*Certo*," he answered fervently. "You will see nothing more of these men sent by him. On this, I have his word."

"The collar will be returned to him, of course; the sooner, the better. You agree, Bella?"

His sister lifted an indifferent shoulder.

"Thank you, my heart," Rico said fervently. "In return I swear to replace this collar with another. It may not have diamonds, but will certainly be a fine substitute."

Bella was silent as she considered that statement. It seemed another good omen. Andrea turned back to his brother-in-law. "It was good of you to come in person to explain everything, also to trust us with this family secret."

"How could I not after everything that has happened. I knew nothing of what my papa had ordered or I would have stopped it sooner. This I swear. As for the attempt to kidnap Petrarca, I am not so helpless that I need someone to arrange my life for me. Nor am I a man who would want his wife to come to him in grief, fear and trembling."

"Fear and trembling?" Bella demanded as her face flushed with outrage. "That will never happen, this I tell you to your face! You have no more idea of what I am like as a woman than your old cretin of a father. You live in the last century, thinking you can explain everything and I will be putty in your hands. Why I ever married you in the first place is a great, great mystery!"

"You married me because I loved you desperately, my heart, and still do. You must listen to what I say now, for it is the truth! You are my one and only love and I have not looked at another woman since the day I first saw you. If you will but hear me, you must be convinced."

"I don't have to be convinced of anything," Bella said, crossing her arms over her chest and glaring at him.

"But you will listen, yes? This time, you will listen?"

It seemed best to give Rico the privacy to plead his case, Andrea thought. Catching Dana's eye, he tipped his head toward the steps that led down to the beach.

It was a relief when she rose, set Guaio on the floor and then moved with composure to join him. And yet something purposeful in her movements, combined with how quiet she had been during the turbulent exchange just past, made him wonder if he had made a mistake.

NINE

The estrangement between Andrea's sister and her husband was as good as over; Dana could see that easily enough. Bella was not the kind of woman to make it easy for Rico, but she seemed impressed by the way he flown to the island to make matters right. Her face had softened as he made his impassioned declaration of love, also. There was no reason they should not reconcile.

Andrea's recounting for her of Rico's explanation seemed to make sense. That he was inclined to accept it was also telling since he knew his sister's husband well.

"How could Rico's father think he could get away with what he did?" she asked as they strolled with the sea breeze lifting her hair and fluttering the long skirt of her sand-colored shift around her legs. "This is the twenty-first century, after all."

"He is not young as Rico was the child of a second wife. He clings to the old ways and hardly knows the century has changed. Or at least he prefers not to admit it."

"But to use such tactics—it's like something out of a movie."

Andrea lifted a shoulder. "They don't make movies from nothing."

"And this is the end of it? I mean, will nothing be done about all that happened?"

"Where is the proof?" Andrea gave a slow shake of his head. "It was as Rico said, only a father trying to help his son, a question of love carried a little too far."

"A little?"

His smile was wry. "Well, more than a little. But Rico is family, you know. How am I to accuse his papa or testify against him?"

"That's a very forgiving attitude." It was also one that seemed very Italian to her, as did his loyalty to family. She could appreciate it now where she might not have a few days ago.

"It's over and no real harm has been done. I prefer to let it rest, unless—"

"Unless?" she asked as he hesitated.

"You wish, perhaps, to press charges?"

Become involved in a court case in Italy? She would have to return for it, no doubt. And though there was a certain appeal in the thought, she knew it would be best not to use it as an excuse. "I don't think so, no."

"Rico will reimburse you for everything that was lost, including any charges not covered by insurance on the rental car. I will see to it."

She didn't doubt him, especially with the set, determined look on his face as he gazed out to sea. "You've already replaced my clothes. It's you he should reimburse for those."

"That was nothing."

The wind stirred the waves of his hair, lifted the collar of his linen shirt against his jaw that he had donned again for lunch. He narrowed his eyes against it, so his lashes meshed at the corners. She wanted always to remember him like this, a part of the sun, sand and sea, sun-bronzed and incredibly male in contrast to the soft white linen he wore, but concerned for her, ready to make everything right for her.

She took a deep breath, steeling herself for what must come. She wished it could be avoided, but knew that was impossible. This had been only an interlude, passionate and life-changing in its way, but never meant to last. Bella's arrival, and Rico's, spelled the end.

It would be best to face that and get it over and done. Waiting for him to say the words was unfair, and would only hurt more in the end.

"So this is it," she said quietly.

He turned to her as if his thoughts had been far away. "What?"

"The danger is over. No one is after Guaio any longer. Or me, if it comes to that. There's no reason for me to stay here."

"No reason," he repeated blankly.

She looked away from the darkness in his eyes. "It's time

I rejoined my friends in Positano. I could take the ferry back to the mainland, except I have no way to pay the fare."

"No."

"No?" she repeated with a species of hope caught in her chest.

"There is no need to rush away. You must stay here while I make these financial arrangements for you."

He only meant to be helpful, as always. She should have known. "You don't have to bother. I can call my parents, and they'll take care of it. I only need a small loan until—"

"*Per Dio*. If you must go, I will take you."

"You don't have to do that. I can make my own way."

He made a brief, chopping gesture. "I'm sure you can, but I will not allow it. I brought you here and I will take you back."

Her throat ached, and there was a hard lump in her chest where her heart should have been. To say anything more was almost impossible, but she managed a single word.

"Fine."

"Fine, then. We will take the helicopter. It will be faster."

Faster was good. That way, the parting would not be so long and drawn out. "I—will be ready whenever you are."

She turned away. Half-blinded by wind, tears and the painful finality of it all, she started toward the stairs that led back to the villa.

"Dana?"

She stopped but didn't turn back. Explaining why she was crying was the last thing she wanted to do.

"You need not go."

His voice, so low and vibrant, was nearly her undoing. She gave a small shake of her head. "I think I do. My friends will be expecting me, and—and the sooner I am with them, the better it will be."

"But there are things between us. We must talk."

She brushed aside strands of hair blown across her face by the wind, felt a warm tear slide down her cheek as she remembered Andrea doing the same thing for her after they made love. "What is there to say? Let's just—just leave it."

"There is this, that I used no protection last night. I would not have you face any consequences from this great stupidity of mine with no one beside you."

"So you would want to be told if there is to be a baby?" He was concerned for a child of his blood, but not necessarily for its mother.

"Of course, *cara*. I should have had more care for this possibility."

"You should, but you weren't alone, you know."

"You had nothing when you came here, so could do nothing. I did, and should have used it."

She could hardly argue with that. "I will let you know if anything happens, but I doubt it will. The timing is wrong."

"You would not—"

"No, I wouldn't." She would never lie to him about such a thing, nor would she even think of destroying his child. It was not only a moral issue but the fact that she couldn't, not when she so longed for that warm and loving reminder.

"*Bene.* I will give you my phone numbers for here, the

mainland and my cell, all of them."

"Yes. Thank you." She couldn't take any more, had no use for a postmortem, no wish to hear any more apologies or expressions of remorse.

She had no regrets. None. In spite of everything.

"I will see you in a few minutes, then," she said, her voice little more than a croak. Moving quickly, almost running, she mounted the steps to the terrace, leaving him there on the beach.

At the top, she paused, however; she couldn't help herself. She had to look back to see if she could make out anything of what he might be feeling.

He wasn't watching her go, not at all. He had taken out his cell phone and was flicking the screen, thumbing numbers.

She faced forward again and walked on, though she could not see where she was going.

~ ~ ~

What to take? Nothing.

What to leave? Everything.

That was how Dana felt. The clothing Andrea had bought for her was too expensive for who and what she was. She would feel odd wearing it around Caryn and Suzanne.

More than that, it was a reminder she didn't need, not while the ache of leaving was so sharp. If her belongings had not been recovered from the rental car, she would borrow from her friends until she could have money sent from home to buy cheaper clothes.

It would be all right. It would have to be all right.

There was little to be packed then. She gathered up her toothbrush and other personal articles out of the bathroom and wrapped them in her nightgown, since she might need that before she could go shopping. Stripping off the linen dress, she put on the jeans, T-shirt and sneakers she'd been wearing when she arrived.

As she started to the close the armadio, she noticed the tiny turquoise bikini Andrea had ordered for her. She'd never worn it for him. If she had remained another day or two, she would have, had planned on it. She'd so wanted to see the look on his face when she whipped off the sarong that was its matching cover-up.

No, she wouldn't think of that. The time might come one day when she could recall the green depths in his eyes, the way they crinkled at the corners when he smiled or lighted up with laughter, without this throbbing anguish in her heart. It wasn't possible now. Not now.

The days had been so few. It seemed more, maybe because so much had been crowded into them. She and Andrea had passed through moments of anger and remorse, danger and passion, yes, but also many that were light-hearted. They had weathered them all and come out safe on the other side.

Well, almost safe, if she didn't count losing her heart. She hadn't meant to fall in love, had never really considered it possible when she boarded the plane for Italy. Oh, she had joked with Caryn and Suzanne about an Italian fling, but she'd thought she was too practical, too armored in the suspicion instilled by her job to actually venture into such a thing. She'd certainly never thought she'd find a man who could undo her with a smile or single soft word.

She would get over Andrea. She would. One day. But she didn't think she'd ever be the same. Some grim, hard element had gone from her life. She'd taken on a degree of the softness of this Italian island in the Mediterranean, the feeling that life was made to be lived, to be enjoyed instead of merely endured as a duty.

All her life, she had been taught black was black and white was white, and the messy, angst-ridden deeds and emotions of human beings that lay in between made no difference. She couldn't see it that way any longer. It was possible she had lost her occupation then, too, because she didn't know if she could go back and police her friends and neighbors as she had before. That job required a grim ability to decide right and wrong for other people that no longer existed for her.

What else she might do, she wasn't sure, but she felt the strong need of a change. She might look into moving to the Florida gulf coast, to finally owning that house beside the sea. She had come to love the constant presence of endless water beyond her window, its sights and sounds and smells. More than that, it would give her some small sense of connection to know that the water that washed up outside her door might have once, for a brief moment, touched the shore where Andrea walked.

Enough.

She wouldn't be maudlin and self-pitying. Pride

required that she hide her hurt, put on a carefree smile. Andrea no more intended what had happened between them than she had. He'd made no promises, held out no hope beyond the few days of this island holiday. He didn't deserve to be made the villain for not offering more.

It was his fault for bringing her here in the first place, however; she couldn't forget that. Still, she had forgiven it. That was only fair, as she wouldn't have missed that unexpected chopper ride for anything in the world.

Picking up her bundle, she gave one last look around the room. She wanted to remember its hand-woven rug, ancient armadio and high bed covered with white and green linens. And dear Guaio, too, who had escaped from his mistress and sneaked in unnoticed, so now lay on the bed watching her with an unblinking stare.

It was then that Dana heard the whining roar of the helicopter engine. Andrea was already preparing for takeoff; she must have been longer than she thought. She would need to hurry if she didn't want to keep him waiting.

She was at the door with her hand on knob when the noise of the chopper altered pitch. Seconds later it changed again, as if the helicopter was lifting off.

That couldn't be.

Could it?

Swinging around, Dana ran toward the balcony door that was still locked and shuttered from the sirocco. She flung back the curtains, struggled with the lock and then with the bar on the shutters. Slamming both open finally, she stepped outside.

The helicopter was hovering above the helipad, rising higher every second. The wind of its whirling rotors blew around her where she stood. As she watched, unbelieving, it reached the apex for flight and then surged forward. It banked, turning in a wide, steady arc before heading for the mainland.

Andrea was piloting it, for she saw him clearly. He noticed her on the balcony as well, for he stared down far longer than he should.

He wasn't alone. Bella was with him, and a shadowed form on the other side of her appeared to be Rico.

They had left her.

Yes, and they'd left Guaio, too, she realized as the cat thumped to the floor behind her and padded out onto the balcony to wind around her ankles. They had been deserted.

She picked up the cat, holding it to her for the comfort of its warm, furry body against the ache in her chest. Standing quite still, she watched until the chopper was no more than a black dot in the sky.

Andrea had left her on the island after saying he would take her to Positano.

He had left her, and she had no idea when or if he meant to return.

TEN

A ndrea scowled through the windscreen as he sent the helicopter hurtling toward Naples. He couldn't wait to drop off his sister and her husband so he could get on with his main objective.

The two of them had not been hard to persuade to leave with him. It seemed they had come to an understanding while he and Dana had talked on the beach. Even now, they were so wrapped up in each other back there on the rear seats that they might have forgotten where they were or what they were doing.

That was just as well. Andrea was in no mood to talk. Not that he was any more interested in watching them exchange the long, hot kisses that were uncomfortable reminders of other things. He avoided those, as much as possible, even glancing toward the back.

He thought of Dana, watching him as he took off without her. She had looked so alone, seemed so disbelieving with her face turned up to the sky. She would learn his purpose as soon as he could manage it. Whether she would forgive him was something else again.

He hated it had to be this way. Still, he could see no other course. To take her to the mainland and leave her, just like that, was intolerable. He wouldn't do it.

She'd thought him arrogant and high-handed before, when he had spirited her away to his island home. She didn't know the half of it.

At least she had Guaio for company. Bella seemed to have forgotten her beloved pet in the rush to leave. Andrea had not reminded her. The cat was better on the island where he could no longer be a bone of contention between her and Rico.

Guaio might be some small consolation for Dana until he returned, but not enough, never enough. He needed to get back to the island as soon as possible.

Naples appeared on the horizon, a gray smudge against a landscape of sea blue and earthen brown. He set the chopper down at the Naples heliport, pausing only long enough to accept Rico's apologies one last time and salute his sister on both cheeks in a fond *arrivederci*. Well before the pair of lovebirds reached the limousine that had been ordered, he was back in his cockpit. As soon as he had clearance, he took off again.

In Positano he took advantage of the helipad owned by a friend who ran a luxury helicopter service between Naples and the town. Moments later, he was behind the wheel of a borrowed car, dodging August traffic in that Amalfi Coast tourist mecca.

The number Dana had called a few days before was stored in his cell phone. All he'd had to do was call it and pretend to represent the rental agency Dana had used, saying he needed to deliver items recovered from the wrecked car. Her friend Caryn had been wary at first, but he was able to provide enough detail to allay her suspicion.

Dana's two friends did not answer the door at the villa. He found them at the pool behind it, stretched out on recliners with their faces shaded by broad-brimmed hats, sun glasses over their eyes and frosted drinks beside them.

"I see you have discovered the joys of our limoncello," he said as he stopped a few feet away.

They sat up as he came nearer. One was short, blonde, blue-eyed and curvaceous, the other dark-haired, rail-thin and exotic. Both were suspicious.

The blonde whipped off her sun glasses, the better to inspect him.

"And who might you be?"

"I am Andrea Tonello, a friend of Dana's."

"Dana doesn't have any friends in Italy." The dark-haired girl watched him with a frown between the winged brows above her chocolate-brown eyes.

"She did not when she arrived." He tipped his head in acknowledgement. "Now, she does. I called a short while ago about delivering her belongings?"

"Funny, but I don't see them."

He gave them his most forthright smile. "No. There has been a slight change of plans."

"Where is she? Why isn't she with you if you're such a good friend?"

That was the blonde, who sat up and reached for a terry-cloth robe to cover her bikini. She could not know that, attractive though she might be in her miniscule white suit, Andrea preferred maillots these days.

"She is waiting on the island," he answered. "I have come to take you away at once to see her."

The pair looked at each other. When they turned back to him, there was no relenting in either face. "What island? Where?"

"My island actually, a private one no great distance out there." He spread a hand in the direction of the sea.

"Yours." The dark-haired girl's voice was flat and quite unimpressed, probably because she didn't believe him.

"Mine, I promise you. It has belonged to my family for many centuries."

"And we're supposed to accept what you say, just like that?"

Instead of answering, he asked, "Which of you is Caryn and which is Suzanne? Wait, allow me to guess." He smiled at the blonde. "You are Suzanne, I think."

Suzanne glanced at Caryn. "At least he must have talked to her."

"And what else," Caryn said, narrowing her large dark eyes. "What have you done with her?"

"Caryn!" Suzanne said in protest.

"What?" the other girl demanded, turning on her friend. "All we heard from Dana is that something happened, an accident of some kind, that she would be delayed but would tell us all about when she saw us. Now this."

"Well, somebody has to know where she's been all this time," Suzanne answered. "Why not him?"

Andrea thought he could warm to the small blonde, though he was less enamored with the brunette. Still, he was pleased to see that Dana had two such protective, caring friends. It made success for what he was about to do seem more promising.

"I see I must tell you everything," he said, his expression grave. "There was an accident, as you were told, but there was more to it than that."

"I knew it!" Suzanne exclaimed. "Dana's not hurt, is she?"

"By no means. She merely became involved in a family quarrel through no fault of her own. It was clearly necessary to provide protection for her."

"Are you sure we're talking about the same Dana?" Caryn demanded. "The one I know can pretty much take care of herself."

"I would agree up to a point," he answered with a wry smile, "especially now. But I did not know her that well in the beginning. Even if I had, the risk was more than I could allow."

"More than you could allow? For Dana?"

Once more, he side-stepped the issue. "That is behind us. Now Dana has need of her friends. You are comfortable here, I can see, but you could be even more so on the island. You would have free run of the property, a village to explore, and a beach mere steps away that is as private as it gets."

"And you're offering all this to us—why? I mean, why not just bring Dana here where she's supposed to be? Why rope us in on this deal?"

He took a deep breath because this was the crux of the matter, the thing he needed of them. "If she leaves, she may never return. If you come to her, she may stay for your sake if for no other reason. She could remain at least as long as your holiday lasts."

Suzanne was watching him, her gaze penetrating. Then a smile curled one corner of her mouth. "You don't want her to leave your island."

"No, I just—" He lifted a hand and then let it fall. "No."

"Well, well," she said with soft intrigue in her voice as she swung to share a long look with Caryn. The two turned back to look at him again.

"Two weeks," Caryn said while speculation sat on her severe features. "That's all we had, and several days are already gone."

"Perhaps an extension can be arranged," he suggested. "It would cost you nothing, you understand, so your funds may last longer."

There was more, though he prevailed in the end. But of course he had to wait in a frenzy of impatience while Dana's friends showered, changed and packed. To expedite matters, he canceled the remainder of their rental on the villa and saw to it the total charge was billed to him. He wasn't sure their luggage, so heavy it might have held iron bars, would not put them over the helicopter's weight limit, but they made it by a hair.

The sun was coasting down the sky by the time they were airborne. Andrea, watching it descend, felt his heart sink as well. Dana had been virtually alone at the island for some time now. He would be lucky if she spoke to him when he landed. The last thing she would do was welcome him home.

~ ~ ~

The first person to step out of the helicopter was a woman. Dana watched that careful descent with her bottom lip caught between her teeth. That was until she recognized the shapely calves, platform sandals glittering with sequins, and petite figure in crop pants and a lime green shirt tied under the bust. Those things added up to only one person.

"Suzanne!"

She almost stumbled on the steps as she pelted down from the terrace and ran headlong across the lawn. By the time she reached the helipad, Caryn had appeared, looking her usual svelte self in a black jumpsuit with a leopard belt. Dana caught them both in the same hug, holding tight. She hadn't seen them since before she left the States. A time or two lately, she hadn't been sure she'd ever see them again.

"What are you doing here?" she cried, releasing them as she saw Andrea waiting behind them. He looked more than a little harassed after time spent with her friends, which might have been amusing if she wasn't so grateful to him. "How did you— I mean, I know how, but—"

"We were abducted," Suzanne said with laugh. "Weren't we, Caryn? Swept up and transported here by Andrea with hardly a by-your-leave. One minute were looking at each other and thinking he was crazy, and the next we were off!"

"He just came and got you?"

The question was directed toward Caryn, but she met Andrea's eyes as she asked it. He appeared uneasy and a little flushed, as well he might.

"Just like that," Suzanne said with a low laugh that held a trace of amusement. "He walked up to us and said he'd come to take us away."

Caryn took Dana's hands, however, swinging them a moment. "He said you needed us."

Stupid tears burned Dana's throat and rimmed her eyes, though she tilted her chin to keep them from falling. "That was—very thoughtful of him."

"Wasn't it," Caryn said, shaking back her dark hair, though there was speculation in her voice.

Dana met the rich green of Andrea's eyes again for a moment, but they gave nothing away of what he thought or felt. Still, it caused him to clear his throat and glance at the other two before he spoke.

"If you will pardon me, I will see that guest rooms are made up, and also send Tommaso for the luggage. Please make your way into the house, all of you, when you are ready."

They watched him go. Dana because she didn't understand what he was doing, the other two with unconcealed admiration.

"Oh. My. God." Suzanne heaved a breathy sigh. "I'm not quite sure where you found him, Dana honey, but you did good! I do believe he may be the most gorgeous hunk of manhood I've seen in my life."

Dana had to agree though she wasn't entirely sure she liked hearing Suzanne say it.

"And he comes with his own private island. All I can say is wow. Wow. Wow."

"We get it, Suzanne, he's something else." Caryn's lips twisted. "Just what, I'm not sure yet."

"What do you mean?" Dana knew she sounded defensive but couldn't help it.

"Pay no attention to her," Suzanne said with a wave of one hand. "She thinks he's too handsome for his own good, as if there could be such a thing."

Caryn didn't bother to reply to that. "I don't know that I believe his story, for one thing. Though I have to say you look as if being kidnapped agrees with you."

"It wasn't like that, not really."

"No? Well how was it then?" Caryn linked arms with her and turned toward the grouping of lounge chairs on the terrace. "We want to hear all about it, every single second, minute and day."

It didn't quite come to that, but was close. Dana left out the more personal parts, though she feared, seeing the wry smiles exchanged by her friends, that they were able to read between the lines. Suzanne and Caryn asked few questions, but they were the right ones. They wanted to know if she was all right, if anything had happened they should know about or that she didn't want. Also if they were intruding, or if she was all right with them being there.

Dana was glad to have them with her, of course she was. She was delighted Andrea had decided to share his island with them. She was pleased they were impressed by it, exclaiming over the Olympic-sized pool, the villa that commanded the island from its hill and the endless vista of the sea. She looked forward to showing all of it to them, also to long days of soaking up the sun and sea air. It was what they had talked about, dreamed about when they set out for Italy, though never in such a luxurious setting.

Yet the fact that they were at the villa was something of a mystery. She had no idea what Andrea meant by it. The two of them had said their goodbyes. What had been between them was over. They were supposed to go their separate ways instead of prolonging the agony.

What did he want from her while her friends were on the island? Did he intend to continue where they left off, making love whenever and wherever? Or would he become the perfect host, seeing to the comfort of his guests with no expectation of more.

It almost seemed it would be better if she was alone with him. She had grown used to speaking her mind whenever she pleased. It chafed her to be prevented from doing it now, also to be compelled by good manners and friendship to sit talking of everything under the sun except the questions that burned in her mind.

Of course, Andrea might not intend to stay now that her friends were here. He could easily fly away and leave them on the island without explaining himself at all.

Tommaso, grinning shyly at the American ladies, came from the house to bring in the luggage. Luisa emerged to tell Suzanne and Caryn that their rooms were ready and they must feel free to rest before dinner, to swim or enjoy a drink on the terrace. The meal would be late by their standards so there was ample time for any of the diversions offered.

Dana went inside with the other two to see the rooms allotted them and make certain they had all that they needed. She might have stayed talking, but caught a glimpse of Andrea from the guest room balcony. He was leaving the house and terrace, walking down the steps toward the beach.

With a quick promise to join Caryn and Suzanne in the living room when they had freshened up, she went quickly back out, moving in the direction he had gone. Guaio, grooming his feet at the top of the steps, turned his head to watch her pass and then got up to glide soundlessly after her.

Andrea stood in the cove with his hands thrust into his pants pockets, staring out to sea. The last rays of the setting sun turned the white outfit he wore to shades of gold and rose, orange and bronze. It gilded him like an ancient Roman statue of the kind they painted to be life-like yet that were larger than life.

She paused for a moment, struck anew by the unreality of being there with him, of being in love with someone so alien, so different from anyone she had ever known or ever thought to know.

That was until Guaio twined around her ankles, rubbing against the legs of her jeans.

Until Andrea turned and saw her, and his lips curved into a smile.

"Everything is all right with your friends?" he asked, his voice deep and beautifully accented against the backdrop of the whispering waves.

"It seems so. They are most impressed and ecstatic to be your guests."

"Even Caryn?"

Her smile was brief. "Even Caryn, at least underneath."

"And you? You are happy?"

"I'm glad to see them, if that's what you mean. It was incredibly thoughtful of you to arrange it." She paused. "But I don't quite understand. Why did you do it?"

He hunched a shoulder without quite meeting her eyes. "You were on your way to have a holiday with your friends when we met. You can do that as well here as in Positano. You said you were anxious to see them, and so I brought them to you."

"Andrea," she said with exasperation, "you can't go around abducting women just because you think you know where they need to be."

"No?"

"No! " She had already answered him before she saw the smile that lurked in the depths of his eyes.

"But *cara*, your friends could not wait to join you after I explained everything to them. They were worried about you, so worried they were almost ready to go to the police. This makes it a good thing I went to Positano."

"Maybe, but I could have set their minds at rest by going to them instead."

His face turned grim. "You wanted to go."

"I was never supposed to stay!" she cried in frustration at her failure to get through to him.

"Because I abducted you instead of asking you politely to come and stay with me? You are the only woman I have abducted, *cara*. You, alone. And I'm not sorry for it. You were safer here. Admit it."

"Well, yes, all right. But don't you see that makes no difference? I don't belong here. I-I never did."

"But you could if you wished it. This could become the house beside the sea for which your heart yearns."

She was unbearably touched that he had been listening, really listening, when she spoke of that dream, also that he had remembered it.

She was also afraid to accept his meaning, so afraid she could be wrong.

"Andrea—"

"You wanted to leave here, wanted to leave me," he went on with a hint of anger rising in his voice. "I thought you might stay longer if I brought your friends. It would give us time to know each other better, perhaps time to care."

He had not wanted her to go. Her throat closed tight so it was impossible to speak as she recognized that much. She could only gaze at him while the wind ruffled his hair, teasing errant strands free so they fell forward onto his forehead.

"I know it has all been too fast, too furious with all that has happened. We are from different countries, different places, and different lives. You barely know me, and what you have seen has not been all that good."

She made a small sound of protest, but he disregarded it as he went on. "I have been as you said before, arrogant and too fond of having my own way in everything." He raked his fingers through his hair and then clasped the back of his neck. "Given time, I might change your mind, might show you more of who I am and how much we are the same despite the differences. But I can't do that if you go away and forget me."

"As if I could," she said on a watery chuckle.

"It isn't funny," he said with a scowl.

"It is to me. Oh, Andrea, don't you know you are unforgettable?"

He watched her for long seconds, his eyes growing darker while his face either changed color or else the sunset painted it. Finally, he said, "You are saying—does this mean you don't mind staying? I am forgiven for going away today without you after saying I would take you with me?"

"Of course. I would have stayed earlier, you know. All you had to do was say you wanted me."

"Oh, I want you, *cara*, more than I want life itself," he said, taking a hasty step toward her. You are my *tesoro*, my heart's treasure, my love who makes my life complete. Without you, I cannot live, nor will I try, not if I have to move heaven and earth to keep you beside me. *Ti amo*, I love you, Dana. I said this to you once, but you did not understand, and then—"

"And I have loved you from the moment you walked out of the mist on the coast road, Andrea. I love that you're different, so very Italian, and even love that you are so arrogant and certain of what you want that you take it as a right. I love you, and want only to be with you."

His face reflected the last light of the sun that was dipping lower into the sea as he swept her into his arms. He held her close and his kiss was warm, tender and filled with promise. And he did not let her go as he whirled with her over the sands with the wind in their hair and the night shadows gathering around them.

Until he stopped, lifted his head.

"Perhaps an evening swim, *tesoro*? You would like that?"

She would indeed, but saw the need to be practical. "Now? But what of Caryn and Suzanne waiting for us on the terrace? And what of bathing suits?"

"Your friends are lovely ladies, but I do not invite them," he said with laughter shining in his eyes.

"No?"

"No." His voice was firm. "Perhaps I will send for friends of mine, Italian heartthrobs so you would say, to entertain them while they are here so I may be alone with you."

"Who told you—"

"Your friend Suzanne, who else? She thought it should be part of her entertainment while here, and I agree."

"She would!"

"Yes. But for now, I see no need for suits for our swim. It is a private beach and almost dark. Do you not agree, *cara?*"

He was irresistible in that mood, or at least he was to her. He wanted her, only her, and that was all she needed. Smiling into his eyes with daring of her own, she gave him the answer he wanted. "Yes, I do agree. With all my heart."

With a shout of triumph, he stripped off his shirt and flung it on the sand. His pants followed, and her shirt, jeans, and all the rest. He picked her up again and ran splashing into the sea while Guaio retreated from the water droplets and then sat on guard with his tail curled around his feet.

They cavorted then, free and a little wild in their joy. He dove around her, sliding along her body. He cupped her, caressed her until she was breathless with need. He caught her, turned to his back and drew her along the firm, slick lines of his body with its faint abrasion of hair here and there.

"I will be our dolphin if you will ride, *cara,*" he said, his voice deep and true.

She smiled at the thought while daring rose inside her. Still, she hesitated. "I would drown you."

"It is a chance I am willing to take."

Irresistible.

"If you are sure."

She eased upon him, taking him inside her. He was an amazing combination of cool and hot, though he was soon as warm as she was where she held him. He took her mouth, surging backward with her, staying afloat she knew not how as her senses melted away along with all consciousness of her body.

Once they sank beneath the waves, kissing still in the swirling blue depths. Rising again, they breathed and laughed, and he whispered in her ear, his smile against her face.

And free, beguiled and infinitely loved, Dana rode.

END

Did you miss any of the other
ITALIAN BILLIONAIRES romances?

THE TUSCAN'S REVENGE WEDDING
(Book 1 in The Italian Billionaires Collection)

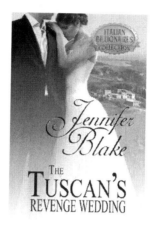

Revenge can indeed be sweet...

When her brother's car plunges off a cliff with him and his fiancée in it, Amanda Davies gets the news personally from the fiancée's brother. The devastatingly handsome Italian businessman appears in Atlanta and whisks Amanda off to Italy to be with the hospitalized couple. But could his motive be more?

Nicholas de Frenza never approved of his sister's choice in husband to begin with, and now that Carita is in a coma due to her fiancé's reckless driving, it seems the perfect time to resurrect an ancient Italian custom of revenge: the seduction calls for a similar seduction in return, a sister for a sister. But Nico is too civilized for such vengeance—or is he?

Even as Amanda falls for the Tuscan's charms, she knows his code and his family would never approve of her as more than a simple dalliance. But then the secret about the car wreck comes out—and that's when everything changes...

THE VENETIAN'S DARING SEDUCTION
(Book 2 in The Italian Billionaires Collection)

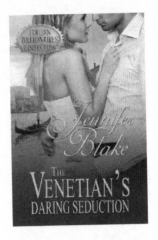

Celina inherited both the cottage where her beloved grandmother painted her famous watercolors and a faded journal that hints at a long-ago Venetian love affair. It's the priceless Canaletto hidden away with the journal that piques her curiosity, however. An art historian and appraiser, Celina can't rest until she knows the story behind the painting—and how deeply the past owner, Conte Massimo di Palladino, touched her grandmother's life.

Lucca Palladino doesn't trust the lovely American who appears at the palazzo, particularly when he realizes his grandfather is smitten on sight. He'll use any means, fair or foul, to remove Celina, including the seductive pleasures of a midnight gondola ride. All he has to do is avoid being seduced himself...

About the Author

National and international bestselling author Jennifer Blake is a charter member of Romance Writers of America and recipient of the RWA Lifetime Achievement Award. She hold numerous other honors, including the "Maggie", the Holt Medallion, Reviewer's Choice, Pioneer and Career Achievement Awards from *RT Book Reviews Magazine*, and the Frank Waters Award for literary excellence. She has written 73 books with translations in 22 languages and more than 35 million copies in print worldwide.

After three decades in traditional publishing, Jennifer established Steel Magnolia Press LLC with Phoenix Sullivan in 2011. This independent publishing company now publishes her work.

FMI: http://www.jenniferblake.com.

You can also find Jennifer on Facebook, Twitter, and Pinterest.

Find Jennifer's books on Amazon at
http://www.amazon.com/Jennifer-Blake/e/B000APHHS8

More Titles by Jennifer Blake

Louisiana Knights Series
Lancelot of the Pines
Galahad in Jeans
Tristan on a Harley
Christmas Knight *(A Holiday Novella)*

Contemporary Romance
The Tuscan's Revenge Wedding
The Venetian's Daring Seduction
The Amalfitano's Bold Abduction
Holding the Tigress
Shameless
Wildest Dreams
Joy and Anger
Love and Smoke

Sweet Contemporary Romance
April of Enchantment
Captive Kisses
Love at Sea
Snowbound Heart
Bayou Bride
The Abducted Heart

Historical Romance

Silver-Tongued Devil
Arrow to the Heart
Spanish Serenade
Perfume of Paradise
Southern Rapture
Louisiana Dawn
Prisoner of Desire
Royal Passion
Fierce Eden
Midnight Waltz
Surrender In Moonlight
Royal Seduction
Embrace and Conquer
Golden Fancy
The Storm and the Splendor
Tender Betrayal
Notorious Angel
Love's Wild Desire
Sweet Piracy

Romantic Suspense

Night of the Candles
Bride of a Stranger
Dark Masquerade
Court of the Thorn Tree
The Bewitching Grace
Stranger at Plantation Inn
Secret of Mirror House

eBOOKS:

Box Sets
Contemporary Collection Volume 1
Contemporary Collection Volume 2
Classic Gothics Collection Volume 1
Classic Gothics Collection Volume 2
Italian Billionaire's TwinPack
Louisiana History Collection Volume 1
Louisiana History Collection Volume 2
Love and Adventure Collection Volume 1
Love and Adventure Collection Volume 2
Louisiana Plantation Collection
No Ordinary Lovers
Royal Princes of Ruthenia
Sweetly Contemporary Collection Volume 1
Sweetly Contemporary Collection Volume 2

Nonfiction
Around the World in 100 Days (with Corey Faucheux)

Novellas
Queen for a Night
A Vision of Sugarplums
Pieces of Dreams
Out of the Dark
The Rent-A-Groom
The Warlock's Daughter
Besieged Heart
Dream Lover

Contact Jennifer Here:
Jenniferblake001@bellsouth.net

Or follow her here:
http://jenniferblake.com
https://www.facebook.com/jennifer.blake.3914
https://twitter.com/JenniferBlake01
http://www.pinterest.com/jblakeauthor
http://www.amazon.com/Jennifer-Blake/e/B000APHHS8

47583246R00139

Made in the USA
Middletown, DE
29 August 2017